I0822886

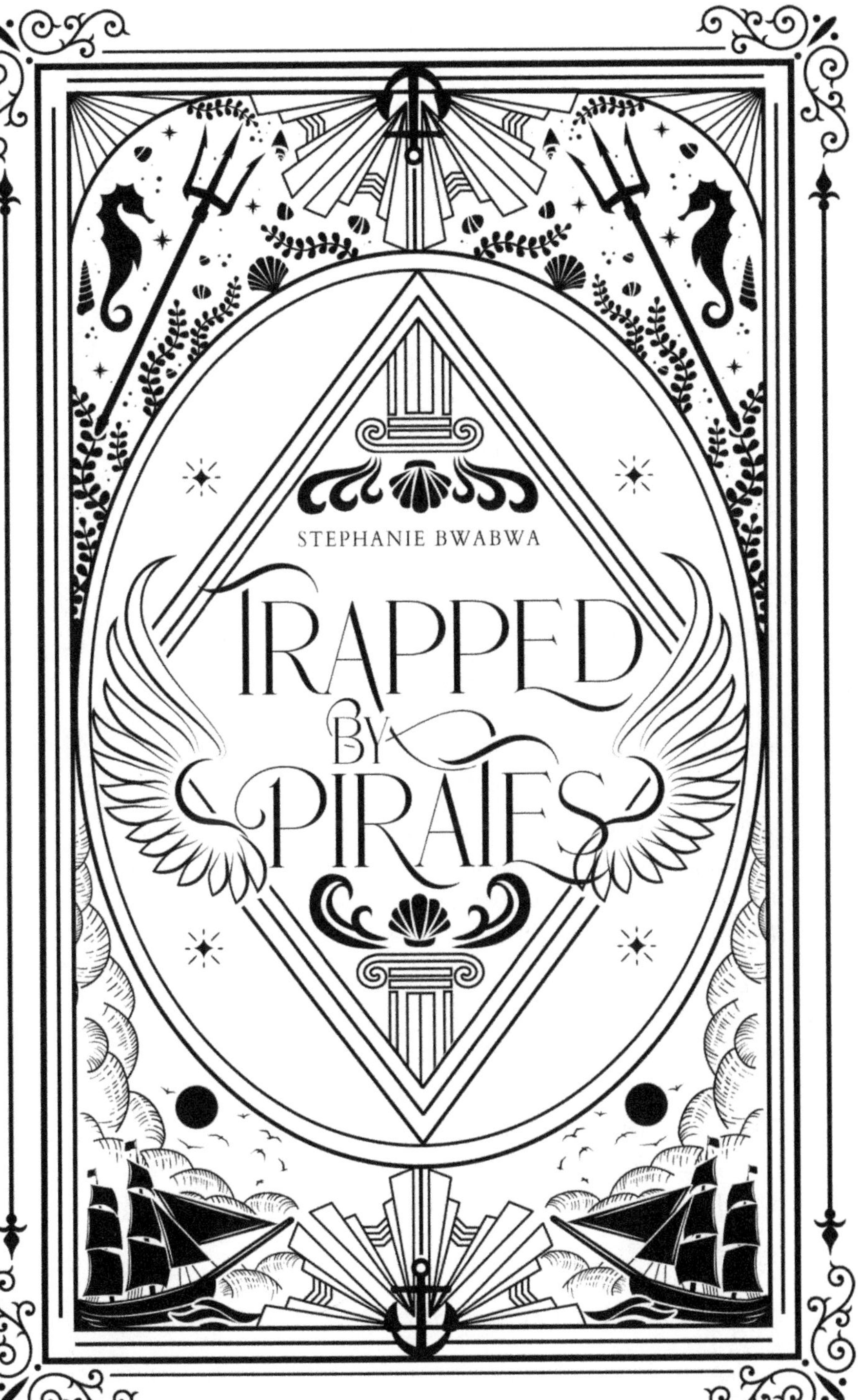
STEPHANIE BWABWA
TRAPPED
BY
PIRATES

This is a work of fiction. Names, characters, places, and incidents are the product of the author's imagination or have been used to create this work of art. Any similarities to actual persons, living or dead, events, etc. is completely coincidental.

Published by: Elledelle Entertainment

www.stephaniebwabwa.com

Trapped By Pirates. 1st ed.

Dust Jacket Cover Design by: Saint Jupiter Graphics

Case Illustration by: Lauren Richelieu Art

Formatting by: Elledelle Entertainment

To the ones who will learn, family isn't who you are born to - it is who you choose to do life with

CHAPTER 1

ALL'S FAIR FOR LOOT AND PRIDE

YAKOBBA

"You weren't expecting to fly away from me alive, were you?"

I dangled my cutlass close to the captain's bleeding ear, gripping his collar in a tightened fist. He squirmed, trying to wedge himself free. I clenched harder while digging the heel of my boot into the tender folds of his wings where I had them pinned.

"Release me."

Spittle flew from the captain's mouth. His two-toned eyes, of pale blue and light gold, stormed beneath the blazing sôlight. Discontented rumbles broke out all over the deck of the ship. Restlessness simmered throughout the shifting feet of my crew as multi-colored eyes embedded in beautiful, hardened faces waiting for me to exact vengeance. I leaned down, bringing myself to a low whisper as I spoke into the captain's ear. Somehow, my voice still carried enough for both crews to hear.

"You'd think with these breeches riding so far up your rhèr, you'd do a better job of riding the sea." I shook his collar. "Yet here you kneel like the skyrat you are."

Snarls broke out among the captain's crew at my insult. I didn't care about any of it. All of them were being held at cutlass-point by my crew. One wrong move and they would lose their heads.

"Clip his wings, captain!"

"Make him fly the plank!"

"Feed him to the octocul!"

Shouts broke out among my crew. I didn't have to look to know who they were coming from. Jaspen, Dakri, and Kassandra. The three eldest in my crew, the first ones to start a fight and the last to know when to quit while they were still ahead.

The captain worked his jaw, his eyes trying to find me. "That's a lot of flower talk from an Avarien bastard who—"

The sudden snap in the air was like a whip against stone. The captain snarled, beginning to foam at the mouth, as Kassandra flew forward, slapping him across the face. Hard.

"Watch how you speak to our captain, fish eater!" Kassandra said, eyes shining wildly.

Urnael didn't.

"You are an embarrassment to Avari," He choked as I twisted my fist in his collar, cutting off his airflow. "A shame to the crown that should be ripped from your head and fed to fish eaters."

Shocked murmurs cut through the thin air surrounding the ship. The earthy-brown faces of my crew darkened, vicious snarls contorting their expressions. The ship remained suspended in the air, balanced in the clouds, skyfuel keeping the vessel airborne.

I swallowed my surprise at the captain's boldness. I sliced off his ear with my cutlass, cutting through bone and sinew. He screamed out, his agony ringing across the clouds. His blood pooled onto my gloved hand, dripping to the wooden deck in leisurely fashion.

"Captain Urnael," I tsked. "You should know better than to push me."

I chuckled darkly. Without blinking, before Urnael could get out another word, I plunged the cutlass into his spine, twisting when I felt the crack of bone. The sound that left Urnael's mouth brought a smile to my face. Excellent lessons taught well always brought about sweet music to my ears.

"If you wanted to pillage angels who traversed the sea to betray the Avarien king," I lifted Urnael's chin with the taloned point of my wing. "You should've done so out of my waters." My eyes flashed. I felt the exhilaration of bloodlust flooding through my veins. "The Mistwind Sea belongs to me. You won't bring the wrath of King Izakaya on our heads. If gossip serves me right, he's demanding a price now," I chuckled darkly. "And it will be paid with your head."

"You don't have the balls to hand my head to the king, Yakobba," Urnael spat, blood and spittle flying. "I have more favor with him than you ever will."

My chest tightened at the insult, and the truth couched inside. I yanked Urnael to his feet and throttled him.

"We'll see how much favor you have when you're dead."

I pushed my cutlass deep into Urnael's bowels. His scream was a broken, agonizing thing. My sword was enough to make him bleed, but it wouldn't end his life. Fuming down out Urnael, I drew on *ethèr*—innate, angelic supernatural, power.

As angels of Domenent rank, we were all Enhancers. My particular affinities allowed me a sort of chameleon ability. I could search out any power around me, tap into the source, and draw on it as if it were my own. As I poured *ethèr* into the cutlass, deeply embedded in Urnael's body, I plunged the power deep, sifting within Urnael's body for his fôrs, his angelic spirit and life energy. Urnael fought back when he realized what I planned to do.

The captain threw up barriers. Wrapped all his defenses with his own powers to throw me off. Kick me out of him.

But I was relentless.

It wasn't long before I dismantled the barriers, with the weight of my *ethèr* flooding his body. As walls inside the angel fall, his fôrs is exposed. Supernatural power pours out from his fôrs to weaken me. Shake me off.

It doesn't.

"Yakobba!" I can hear the captain's anguish.

Hearing the free use of that name angered me. Angered me so much I rushed at his fôrs with unmitigated rage. We did a dance of war, spirit against spirit, but I won. I poured my *ethèr* into Urnael's fôrs, wrapping the ethereal, angelic frame with cords of light and raging brilliance. Then, I squeezed and siphoned out his life force. I can hear Captain Urnael screaming. Pleading for mercy. Begging to live.

He won't.

I squeezed harder, siphoning out every drop of waking existence I found, watching as his fôrs slowly weakened, losing its life, until finally there wasn't a flicker of light that remained. Not another drop of golden light flecked in the expanse within Urnael. Everything grew dim, then dark, until I knew for sure he was dead.

I released my hold, pulled my *ethèr* and cutlass out of him, and looked around. My crew still floated over Urnael's captured crew, their eyes blinking with satisfaction, and their hunger for blood churning. Without bothering with another glance at Urnael's lifeless carcass, I spun around and spread all six pairs of my membranous, feathered, wings wide, and began levitating off of the ship's deck.

The sôl above blazed brilliantly over the clouds. I looked down at where my ship remained on the surface of the Mistwind Sea below. Looking back at my quartermaster, I nodded once, a flame burning behind my eyes.

"Kill them all."

Pleas for mercy broke out among those who still lived from Urnael's crew. I had no taste for prisoners, especially when they proved to be beggars.

Engèli's lips crawled upward, a fiendish grin stretched across his mouth. "And the *Airflower*, Captain Ashthorn?"

I flicked my gaze over the massive vessel that was once an Avari warship. A ship the king of Avari refused to let me step foot on, no matter how much I proved capable of being her captain. Disgust curdled my gut.

"Burn it down."

"Aye!"

Horrendous screams filled the air like sweet music to my ears as I flew down from the vessel, floating gently along the breeze back to my ship.

CHAPTER 2

A BARGAIN WITH THE SEA

RAESHELLE

The sea meandered on as if in mourning. I picked up a bite of kòd fish with my coralsticks and chewed, stifling my rising anxiety. I grudgingly remembered the last time I had a noonfast—the mid-dawn lunch meal—that came with this much mental anguish.

Across from me sat King Bakari Ezrathen Au'Pearl. He sat back in the shellchair with his shoulders relaxed, his six wing pairs lazily brushing through the water, as he drank his seawine with the calm of a fallen god.

There was a reverent quiet in the air as we ate in peaceful silence, the resplendence of the royal gardens our backdrop. A group of youngling angels, seated in gilded saddles atop seastallions, swam by along the outer edge of the Pearl Palace. I trailed them until they disappeared near the Glass Reefs. A pang of envy tugged at my six hearts. I suppressed it, looking back to my kòd. I was a princess, not a common angel. It wasn't for me to go outside of the castle, gallivanting as if I didn't have duties.

"Raeshelle."

I looked up to find King Bakari watching me. His curious eyes loomed just above the rim of his goblet, the pale blue and silver of his irises glistened in the low light of the sea.

"You've left me for a third time. Do I bore you?"

I flushed, instantly squirming in my seat beneath the weight of his moon-like gaze. Few things escaped those eyes. Including falsities. I took another bite of kòd fish, buying time before answering.

"No, my king. You could never." I looked into his eyes, praying my nerves couldn't be seen. Smiling, I leaned forward, waving my coralsticks with nonchalance. "I just love watching the heartbeat of the sea, that's all. Mistwind is beautiful. Each moment I get to be in her presence, I cherish it."

King Bakari said nothing, eyeing me for a long while. After he drank several sips of seawine, I grew nervous. I pressed the length of my skirts beneath the crystal table, digging my nails into the shell embroidery of the eelsilk. I looked away from the king, turning my attention to a school of tuana swimming in the distance.

"My king, hm?"

I snapped straight, sitting up in my shellchair. My mouth dried as I coughed, searching for an excuse.

"I meant no offense by calling you—"

"Payè will suffice, Corellis."

My nostrils flared. I fought down the flood of panic choking out my waterflow, hindering my ability to breathe. It wasn't often he used my middle name. Not since the queen was given to the sea in the Azizien Rite.

"I may be king to Azizi and her angels. But to you," King Bakari pointed a finger at me from the grip still holding his goblet. "I remain, Payè." He tilted his head, still analyzing me, noting my reactions. My response. "Promise me you won't forget that, hm?"

The surrounding water stirred, chilling my body. I breathed it in, letting the ripples pour through my gills, into my lungs, and then through my veins. I was as cold as an iceberg and loving it. Finally, I felt myself relax.

"Yes, payè," I nodded, reaching for my goblet. "I won't forget."

I gave him a sheepish smile, drinking some of the seawine. Blessed seas. It was delicious. A sweet citrus taste with a sparkling tingle danced on my tongue. I licked my lips between sips while fluttering my wings. They moved the surrounding water, causing a flitter of bubbles and small waves. I blinked at the noonfast feast before us, thinking of how to bring up what I really meant to talk about. King Bakari had a full dawn of meetings with his Ministraithe, but canceled them all when I urged the importance of him eating with me this dawn. I didn't want to waste his time.

At the edges of the garden, around the entire circumference, floated the Au'Pearl Seaveillers. Some specifically attended to me, while the rest were payè's personal guards. The Seaveillers of the king were fearsome brutes. Sea-carved machines born and bred for war. Which I couldn't understand, since Azizi was a peaceful nation with no enemies. When their leader, Seaveiller Alaika, caught my attention with her brooding blue and green eyes and scowled, I looked away. That one was never happy. Seeing a smile on her face would be a miracle.

Through my peripheral, I looked at King Bakari

Ezrathen Au'Pearl, my payè, and the Azizi kingdom's fearsome, but beloved, king. As big as he was intimidating, perched in the oversized shellchair, he returned to filling his plate with fish, sea crackers, chilled shells and iced seaweed, patiently waiting for me to get to the point.

I swallowed, trying to find my nerve. I could do this. This was my payè. I could ask him a simple question. This was no big deal.

Except, this was a big deal.

I tried to prepare for whatever reaction he would give. But I still wasn't ready. I sighed, using my coralsticks to push my food around my plate.

"Spit it out, Corellis," he said, eyes still on his plate. "What ails you my dayè?"

I worried my bottom lip, pushing around karraba bites, until I finally spilled.

"I would... Well. I'd like a... quiet riseday this cycle." Playing with the karraba bites, I avoided eye contact. "Just me and you. Maybe even Kianga. Nothing fancy or crazy. It won't require much planning and—"

"No."

The rest of my words dried on my tongue, turning to soot. I didn't even get to finish.

I blinked at him.

King Bakari looked at me with those inquisitive, intelligent eyes piercing into my skull. He hadn't won, and kept the throne for as long as he had by being a fool. It suddenly dawned on me. In the prolonged silence, he'd guessed why I had summoned him, even before he arrived. He flattered me with his presence, but his mind was already set before he'd even sat down. I could feel my hope deflating with each passing moment.

"No."

The note in his tone was final.

"But payè, I—"

"A quiet riseday," he cut in. "You've never asked for such a thing before. You always looked forward to your birthday celebrations. But now you want quiet." He raised a brow. The infinitesimal scales lining his brown skin reflected the shifting colors of the sea in the low light. "Why, Raeshelle? Why do you ask this of me now?" He took a sip from his seawine. "What is it you really want?"

"Payè." I looked him in the eyes, searching for any hint at him budging on his decision. "I want what I said. Something quiet. Something private. I'm older now and don't want all the pomp and noise. I don't want a big celebration—"

"You're lying, and you know how I feel about

such behavior." He pulled himself up to sit straight, shaking off karraba juice from his short, pristinely filed claws. "Tell me the truth or you'll find yourself locked in your chambers for the next mekàd."

A month of isolation? He couldn't be serious. I barely got to go anywhere of my will as it was. Mandatory isolation would be hellish. I straightened, flattening the bunching lines in my well-endowed gown.

"I don't want to go to the Atlanthyst Trench," I blurted out. I bit my bottom lip, fidgeting to keep from leaping out of my seat and swimming away.

"Ah." King Bakari sat back, analyzing me with a shrewd gaze. "Now we reach the searock of it."

Payè looked away, his crown catching the sea's reflection in its jewels. I admired the collection of rare coral and gems interwoven with seavines made of pure gold and starcrystal. King Bakari was as handsome as he was powerful, and feared, above all angels who lived beneath the Mistwind Seas. Azizi was a thriving kingdom because of him.

I traced the features that caused Queen Audriana to say yes to King Bakari. Then he scowled, eyes glued to the sea, and I saw all the reasons I secretly wished she had said no.

"Raeshelle Corellis, my dearest princess."

King Bakari turned to me, resting a weighty stare on my shrinking frame. I looked back, feeling small. Greedy. Foolish.

"You are an Au'Pearl. Will you not face your royal duties like one?"

My stomach knotted with guilt. His words felt like blows. To my gut. My hearts.

My eyes fluttered closed as the stones sank in my stomach and shame filled my blood. Searot. Why did I even bring this up? After all, he was right. The duty of my crown would always supersede my personal need. I felt the tears welling up before I could seal the barrier to my emotions and keep them at bay.

"Come with me, youngling."

Without waiting for me to follow, King Bakari pushed back from the crystal table, shook out his wings—six membranous pairs lined with small scales—and began swimming towards the palace bridge. Slipping from the table, I followed, letting the water current carry my body along the flow so my wings didn't have to work hard. I flew behind the king in silence as several Seaveillers floated behind us. I noticed each one belonged to the king's guard, and not mine. Frowning, I kept my eyes forward.

"Payè, where are we going?"

We swam past a bed of clams the size of newborn dolfinis, their mouths opened with large pearls sitting inside. The pearls emanated a warm light that kept the garden feeling cozy. The king finally answered, and I shivered.

"To the bridge. It's time I show you something."

CHAPTER 3
ENTERING A PIRATES SABBATH
YAKOBBA

The clouds above filled with smoke, as ash turned to rain, tainting the dawn. Balanced atop the guardrail, I floated with anticipation, waiting for Engèli to finish the job and return to the ship. The *Airflower* burned in the skies overhead, her glory charring into undesirable waste. I watched her burn with satisfaction. With every flame that rose, I solidified my name along the Mistwind Seas. It would be long before another captain tested my patience again.

Within the hôr, Engèli and the crew that remained on the *Airflower* made their descent. They did a slow flight of victory, stressed by wide grins and dancing eyes. As the *Airflower* turned to dust, my angels returned to the *Ashweaver*, planting themselves amid the awaiting crew.

I looked at Engèli, raising a brow.

"All clear?"

"Like piss after drinking a barrel of water."

Engèli grinned, the smile reaching from ear to ear. I choked on a rising guffaw forming in my throat. Cackles littered the main deck. Few of the crew just shook their heads looking at Engèli like he was an oversized, brainless oaf.

Among the shaking heads was Nyala Tereth, my second mate. Her round face was scrunched in a mixture of disgust, annoyance, and embarrassment. Nyala shot Engèli a glare.

"Careful, Nya," Engèli taunted. "Keep screwing your face like that and it'll stay that way. You'll go to the Ellelights looking like a stareagles rhèr."

I choked again, struggling to keep from laughing out loud. A burst of laughter to my right threatened to break my resolve. I snuck a peak and found Jabari Zarya, the Gunner of the *Ashweaver* and my third brain, bent over his knees, howling. I took a deep breath, praying to the Alpha to help me keep my composure.

Nyala's flaring temper was a lethal, tangible

thing. She floated closer to Engèli and Jabari, hands swirling with her summoned *ethèr*. She could barely reach the chest of either angel, yet the command in her eyes whittled them to only younglings in need of a good plank to their hides.

"You want something to laugh about rotpots?" Nyala seethed. "I've got something for you."

I rushed to the forefront of the main deck, raising a booted foot to the wooden ledge. I rose my blood-stained cutlass before Nyala could get to my pirates. She was tiny, but she could take them both easily, and win.

Spreading my wings—all six feathered pairs—wide open, I pulsed them twice, a show of power and control, before speaking. The moment I tucked my wings back in, every angel on the ship fell silent, all eyes on me.

"Eya!"

The gathering call bellowed from my throat like a roar. The angels responded by stomping their right feet twice, then slamming one of their wings onto the floor of the deck.

"I've said it before, and I'll say it again. The Mist-wind Sea is ours."

Cheers exploded across the deck as the angels

leapt into the air, pumping their fists, and flying back down to stomp their feet.

"Many have been waiting for us to fail. For us to surrender and beg for mercy. For bread."

"Never!" Jabari cried. "We'd as soon eat our own rot before bending for anything."

"Unless we're bending with a pretty little—"

"Enough," I cut in before Engèli got out of hand. Engèli and Jabari slapped hands, grins showing all of their teeth before they returned their attention to me. Nyala's eyes—one sky blue while the other was a bright aquamarine—bristled under the sôlight as they narrowed at our mates. She crossed her arms, tapping a booted foot while silently fuming at Engèli and Jabari.

"Will you two shut up so we can get off this rotting ship?" She sucked her teeth, looking away. "Childish. So bloody childish."

Nyala muttered something under her breath. I couldn't hear her, but the crew closest to her busted out laughing. As curvaceous as she was hot-blooded, I knew well. Nyala's temper was nothing to tame. I prowled on before she snapped.

"Nya's right. Shut it. We're all ready to be off."

Engèli snorted but grew silent, with Jabari following suit.

"You've got your loot. What's yours is yours. And no, you don't have to share."

A round of cheers broke out among angels who were faster at pillaging Urnael's ship than the rest. The crew, who remained on the *Ashweaver*, and didn't loot at all, grumbled like younglings ready to throw a tantrum. I shrugged them off. They'd get over it.

"Spend it as you wish. Lavish in your pleasures. You've earned it."

A raucous cheer exploded. Even Nyala joined in, spreading her wings and clapping them. As they cheered, I floated down to join them. These angels had been hardened over many cycles. They were forced into living life at sea. They pledged to stay by my side and have proven their loyalty since. I swelled with pride, looking at them as they shouted and danced, ready to cause havoc once they were free of the ship.

The moment the anchors dropped, and we safely docked, I took off, leading the charge. I floated across the connecting ramp from ship to pier, landing on hardened, cloudy earth. My crew followed suit, keeping pace as we split the sea of onlookers in half. Gossip broke out like the plague as soon as the onlookers saw my face.

"Blighted skies! It's him, isn't it?"

"Isn't that the High Prince?"

"High Prince? Fool. He's a bloody pirate, and the worst of them all."

"He is the uncrowned heir."

"As handsome as he is cruel, I've heard he is."

"If he's here, won't be long until the Crown follows."

I ignored them all and continued my languid flight until I came to perch in front of sandy doors, freshly polished, barricading the roar of chatter and lawlessness inside.

"Don't just float there, Cap. Let us in."

Engèli grunted, no doubt his stomach urging him to hurry and satisfy his needs. I chuckled under my breath, shook my head, and pushed the door open. Blaring music blasted my ears. The heavy scent of old skywine flooded my nostrils.

I settled to my feet, striding into the *Darkwing Kiss*. My home away from home. Most especially because it remained unchecked by King Izakaya. I thought of the king and my insides knotted. With yearning? With unrealistic hope? It took effort, but I shoved the emotions down.

A large palm on my shoulder stole my attention. I turned to find Engèli watching me, a sober expression lining his concerned face. His royal and ocean blue eyes were burning.

"He misses you, too, Cap."

"Nothing but rot." I looked away, unnerved at how well Engèli knew me. "Bastard of Avari is my reputation for a reason."

I shook off the suffocating desire for home and forced myself to regain my composure.

"I'm good. A few pints of the wretched stuff and all of this will turn back into what it really is." I looked at Engèli. "Memories."

Engèli frowned, seeing right through my bluff.

"Sure, Cap. If you say so," Engèli suddenly snapped his attention to something behind me. "Look who has been waiting on you, Cap."

I turned and smiled. Across the chamber floated an angel fairer than most found in all of Avari. Her face was round and her skin was bronzed like earth. Her multi-colored green eyes burned with desire, her short frame sauntering towards me leisurely. She was curvy, enticing, and exactly who I wanted to see, and hold, at this moment. As she crossed the tavern, she gave me a small, ensnaring smile that stripped me of breath. Of any present sense.

I was prepared to shoot across the chamber, take

her up into my arms, and fly us somewhere private, when—

"Well now. Look what the dregs of the Black Hells coughed up." A dark chuckle. "If it isn't his Uncrowned Highness, come to grace his peasants for a bit of fun."

CHAPTER 4
TERROR OF THE MISTWIND SEAS
YAKOBBA

A prickling sensation needled the center of my palms. The beat was in tandem with the rhythm of my pounding hearts. I could feel the tantalizing desire to break something heat my blood. I forced myself to breathe. Not all confrontations had to end in a fight, right?

Ominous laughter filled the dimmed chambers of the *Darkwing Kiss*. A chilly flare flittered down my spine, egging on the pulse throbbing in my palms.

Deep breaths, deep breaths, deep breaths, I chanted to myself.

No more fighting this dawn.

I stopped floating midway to the pretty courtesan in scantily clad clothing, covered in my favorite perfumes. I turned to find the idiot dumb enough to start something violent with me and gave him a murderous smile.

"Come again?" I pivoted to face the angel wholly, the hem of my noir cloak dragging along the aged carpet. "I didn't hear you. You'll have to speak louder."

The *Darkwing Kiss* fell quiet. All activity in the tavern skittered to a halt.

I made a note of the seven angels sitting at a long table, leaning back in their cloudchairs lazily, their wings drooping to the carpet. They looked unbothered, bored even. But the glint in their eyes told a different story. Several of them balanced a hand atop their cutlasses, tucked into their waistbands. These angels were as large as Engèli, if not bigger, and equally tall.

The stranger himself was darker than most in the tavern. His eyes glittered like iridescent pearls. Unlike my tall, wiry frame, he was all chiseled bulk with jagged lines branded into his face. Scanning his physique, my eyes snagged on the broken points in his wings. That could only mean one thing.

This angel was a deserter.

A disgraced former Sky Watcher.

"Did I stutter, skyrat?" I tilted my head with the

grace I watched King Izakaya wear his entire reign, and tsk. "You can be loud. You can be dumb. But you're a pitiful excuse for an angel if you choose to be both."

The seven brutes at the table snarled, shooting to their feet, whipping out their cutlasses. In my peripheral vision, I saw Nyala and Jabari doing the same, as they simultaneously summoned their *ethèr*. Engèli sat at an opposite table, eyeing the seven angels, his pale and hazel eyes darkening with each passing moment.

I should have de-escalated this tension. My crew and I just had an altercation that ended in blood. They were hungry, tired, and needed a break. They didn't need to shed any more blood. Cause anymore scenes.

I should've let this go. I should've carried on with the courtesan still waiting for me. Instead, I exposed what the deserter did and insulted him, labeling him worse than the dung of Avarien dogs.

Besides, I was still in the mood for a fight.

The angel who spoke floated to a stand, levitating in the air. He squared his jaw and pulsed his wings in an act of intimidation. I almost laughed. He looked ridiculous. They all did.

"We're not afraid of you down here, High Prince Yakobba."

He laughed bitterly as mounting anger warmed my cheeks.

I suddenly felt exposed.

And ashamed.

The invisible crown above my head threatened to make me go mad.

"You think just because your payè wears the crown I won't still fold you like the little buckling you are?"

Hisses and snarls escaped the lips of my crew. Nyala bursted out in a slew of curses. Jabari used his *ethèr* to form a braided whip around the long, curved blade of his cutlass, his gold and amber eyes glowing dangerously in the dimmed light of the tavern. Engèli casually pushed back from the seat he'd just found, pulled out his cutlass, and drummed a ringed finger on the hilt. He was as much ready for a fight as I was.

I grew silent and unnaturally still.

Buckling.

The image of a youngling being taken against their will, and broken in ways no angel should ever experience, flashed behind my eyes. I shuddered in an icy rage at the insult. I took a deep breath. Let my eyes fall shut.

I ignored my royal title. Ignored my unworn crown. I pushed past the judgement, hatred, and wrath hurled at me. I was once a High Prince, but the king saw fit to break me before I could don the crown. So I left the Cloud Castle and became a pirate. Oily rage snaked through my chest. I thought I had squashed all disrespect at my choice with Urnael. Now I would need to make an example out of this fool.

The ayèn barked out a laugh, his masculine pride on full display.

"Don't tell me the little princeling is scared." Growing laughter washed over me, squeezing my temples, beating at my chest. I felt the peals of laughter sink into my bones, grating on my last nerve. "He's far from home without his little guards, throwing tantrums across Mistwind with hope his payè will finally give him attention. Because he's still a buckling—"

All sound around me grew quiet. I heard nothing as my spirit plane grew dark. An eery melody played in the silence. Then something unhinged in me snapped. I flared out my wings, launched myself forward, and collided with the angel. Hard. His body flew across the tavern, slamming into the end wall of the connected chamber.

Without thinking, I catapulted myself at an angle with my wings still spread wide. Sharpening each feathered point like a blade, I pounced on the crumpled form of the angel and swiped across his torso, cutting through the fabric until I tore into his thick skin. He screamed. His golden blood gushed out of his chest, coating his tunic and breeches, and getting into my clothes and cloak.

The ayèn unwound from his broken position on the floor and shot into the air, almost ramming himself against the ceiling. He raged belligerently. It was a terrifying sight.

I watched him, nonplussed. I blinked, eyeing every exposed pain point on his body where I would unleash unmitigated anguish.

He lunged for me with a wing as he pulled out two crosswords. I ducked, dodged his blows, spun over myself with my wings tucked tight, then flew above him in the chamber. The angels looked on. I noted Engèli, Nyala, and Jabari still watching the angel's lackeys, waiting for them to make a move so they could have a viable reason to drench the carpet with their blood.

I looked back to my opponent, lunged as he tried to dive out of the way, and slammed down the heel of my boot over his head, breaking the skin of his forehead. The crack at his temple barely registered. I barrelled into him again, going for an uppercut. I slapped my wings upside his head, the sound like boulders colliding into mountains. Warm blood trickled onto my knuckles and dripped to my exposed chest in my tunic, but I didn't stop.

I pounded into his head. Rammed my wings into his body. Cut him with the taloned points of my wings like a dagger. Midnight swam in my vision. I lost sight of the *Darkwing Kiss*. I only saw the massive ox of an angel and my relentless need to pulverize him.

I lost track of time.

Of sense.

Of self.

Eventually, something tight inside of my chest deflated. I heaved a sigh, breathing deeply. A firm hand gripped my shoulder. Another pulled me back from an unmoving body crumpled in a heap like dynamited rock. A third pair of hands gently gripped my arms, holding me still.

"Breathe, Cap. Breathe."

I blinked, chest heaving, unable to process where I was. What just happened?

Then I found the pool of blood snaking through the *Darkwing Kiss*. And the mess of a body left contorted in the middle of it.

The tavern was quiet. Music ceased playing. No wings were beating. No one was drinking. All eyes danced between me and the lifeless angel. My eyes fluttered shut. I could hardly face what I'd done.

Images flashed behind my eyes. They were all younger versions of me, locked away in a chamber with King Izakaya, his heavy hand, and his "special tools" needed for discipline. It always happened after I bested my bayè in yet another competition. He didn't take kindly to me embarrassing my brother, and I needed to be taught long, hard lessons as a warning to not do it again.

I shook with a torrent of emotions ripping through my hearts. My mind. I ran away from the monster in the Cloud Castle only to turn around and become him. I breathed heavily, fighting back the sting of restrained tears.

Nyala rubbed my back. She gently brought me from the disheveled chamber into another, sitting me down at a table where others of my crew were waiting. Engèli stayed close behind, eyes scanning the friends of the dead angel, daring them to make a challenge. All seven looked between themselves and their dead friend before rushing out of the tavern, leaving the angel's broken body behind.

"We could use some music in here," Jabari barked.

Instantly, a jovial tune started up. The paid entertainment of the *Darkwing Kiss* launched back into a song as if nothing had just happened.

An extended amount of time passed before I could regulate my breathing. Before I could suppress my anger. Leash my darkness. A mug of skywine was shoved into my hand. I put back the entire mug in three large gulps. It was refilled before I could think to ask for more.

I drank and drank, growing increasingly numb. A familiar touch, dainty but firm, massaged my shoulders. A soft kiss at the winged tip of my ear sharpened my senses. Something unfettered loosed within me.

"Masaiya," I breathed.

My worries deflated, replaced by something else. Something raw and writhing. She nibbled on my ear, tugging. I turned to her, answering her silent demands. My lips crushed against hers, hungry and devouring. I scooped her up in front of all the staring angels in the tavern.

With Masaiya in my arms, I few across the *Darkwing Kiss*, rushing up the spiral ramp to our favorite suite. Before I could reach the chambers, she was singing my favorite melody of pleasure, freeing me of bothersome thoughts about kings, crowns, and courtly creeds.

CHAPTER 5
TRAPPED BY FATE
RAESHELLE

Eyes glued to the enchanting underwater towers rooted to oceanic rock below, I followed King Bakari to the palace bridge distractedly. I fought against the tightening knots twisting in my stomach. More than several cycles had passed since the last time the king brought me to the bridge. We had to swim beyond the palace proper, far past the courtyard into an open waterway that bled out to a drop off.

The Pearl Palace was rooted atop ancient rock protruding from the seabed that rose high like a mountain while all life was encircled around its base. The bridge was the only connection to the entry of the waterway and the Azizien city that lied below.

My entire life, I'd been forbidden from going beyond the palace proper, let alone all the way to the edge of the bridge, unless given permission and under heavy watch by my Seaveillers. I rarely got to see the rest of the sea.

My mind raced with possibilities. What could the king possibly be bringing me here for? What did this have to do with my coming riseday? I wanted to ask him, but I opted for a change of topic, lest I trigger his ire and his brooding temper.

"Azizi is so beautiful. The city beams with its towers of crystal. And look how the shell lamps glow! I love how the light illuminates the city."

King Bakari grunted in agreement, nodding at the bustling life below and beyond.

"A magical world our kingdom is. I couldn't be more proud to be her king."

My hearts swelled with pride at the sentiment. Then immediately constricted. If I didn't go through the Azizien Rite like Queen Audriana, all of this would be poisoned by the Taint and die.

I swam after the king through tall water lilies littered around the base of the sea mountain, upholding the palace. King Bakari swam to the edge of the bridge, found a vacant shellchair, and sat. I swam up beside him and plopped into the shellchair next to his, watching a myriad of fish pods swimming toward their reefs. It took a moment for me to realize what we were actually here to look at. I pressed my lips into a thin line.

"Beyond the city of crystal towers and coral rooftops. After the fish clusters, dolfini and shrark pods, turtu and karraba coves, and stingspray weeds. Past the Boneyard, and beyond the monseriö infested sea, lies..."

"The Atlanthyst Trench," I quipped.

"The Atlanthyst Trench is significant to Azizi because?"

"It is where our hierranks, the Saerels, first gave us the Atlanthyst Stone and commanded us to use its power to heal the waters of the Azizi kingdom, and the waters of the Mistwind Seas."

"And if we do not uphold the generational rituals of the Azizien Rite?"

My shoulders cowered at the weight of his questions. I kept my eyes glued to the Mistwind Sea and all the sea life flowing in her waters. There was a magical touch of life and effortless beauty hanging around the Azizi kingdom. She was perfect, healthy, and whole. For now. The Taint hadn't reached her inner waters just yet. But it would. Soon. I choked on my answer.

"If we bypass the Azizien Rite, we will be forced to succumb to the growing Taint... and the kingdom will die."

The king was silent for a long time. I began fidgeting in my seat, unnerved at his quiet as we watched sea angels swim below, opting to travel by sea-flight than using their water chariots. The angels mingled with the sea life, letting fish pass through and around them, as they themselves swam in and out of those pristine towers.

"You mean to tell me you would sacrifice the entire kingdom... you would allow all of this around us to die because of your greed to live one more cycle? Have I not done everything to give you the best life possible while you still lived to enjoy it?"

My eyelids fluttered shut as I choked down a rising sob. My wings curled in on themselves as I shook with my shame. How could I be so selfish? I had the best example before me. Queen Audriana had the power of the stone placed inside of her. She gave her life so the kingdom would thrive. And here I was hunting for any reason to not do the same.

Tears streaked down my cheeks. It wasn't my desire for our angels, and all the sea life that grew to lean on us for healthy reefs and coves, to die. I just wasn't ready to be the reason they all got to live. I trembled with tears at the wrestling emotions inside of me. Searot. What I wouldn't give to make this incessant desire go away.

"You probably think me cruel."

I shook my head and reached a hand over to take his large, webbed hand, with their finely sharpened claws, into mine. I squeezed the king's hand and forced myself to look into his intelligent, fierce, kind eyes.

"I don't think you cruel, payè. You love me and this kingdom both. You desire to serve our angels as best as you can while doing the best by me, as well. I just wish there was another way. But I'm not naïve. I can clearly see that there isn't."

His eyes crinkled at the corner, his irises softening. He unfurled a wing and wrapped it around my petite frame, tucking me close to his side. I felt hot tears pricking my eyes. I didn't want to be a disappointment to my payè.

But rot.

I couldn't ignore the gnawing hunger in me to live.

King Bakari lifted a hand to hold my cheek. I didn't realize how badly I was crying until I saw the tears dripping down his palm.

"My Pearl. You know, it is a great honor to lay

your life down for the kingdom. You are the greatest, and purest, gift that could ever be given to the sea."

He stroked my cheek with a ringed thumb, gentle eyes smiling at the corners in a way that melted my hearts. He was right. It was my turn to be the salvation of the kingdom. I nodded, shaking off all the other desires.

"That's my Corellis. Azizi will never be more proud than when you will complete the Azizien Rite."

I forced myself to believe his words. At least I tried. But I still couldn't help the truth. Though I was fated to die, I wanted nothing more than the gift to live.

CHAPTER 6
SUMMONS OF THE SKIES
YAKOBBA

The light of dawn flooded the *Darkwing Kiss* as I strutted into the main hall. Laughter turned to curious whispers as I scanned the large chamber, searching for familiar faces. In a corner, with a pillar of cloud shrouding them for privacy, I spotted my crew. Cackling loud, with voices raised in shouts, the angels of the *Ashweaver* berated one another while scarfing down their firstfast. I didn't float two paces their way before Nyala whipped around in her seat, eyes ablaze. I gulped, bracing myself for the lashing.

"Rein in your dogs or I will."

Her voice was deathly calm as storms brewed in the pits of her eyes. Engèli howled with laughter behind her. Jabari quaked, tipping his head back to bark a laugh, himself. I had no clue what they were on about, and something told me to stay out of it.

"Nya," Engèli purred. "I know you'd want to taste at least one—"

"Shut up, cloud eater," she spat, shaking her fist in Engèli's face. "I swear, if you don't shut up—"

Nyala whipped out a wing, whacked Engèli upside his head, and gruffly shoved his massive form out of his seat. The angel tumbled to the floor, still howling to the point of tears. Jabari bent over, snorting into his goblet. He was wheezing now, tears flowing down his mahogany cheeks.

I shook my head.

A cacophony of noise filled the tavern. I looked to see more of my crew, nearly all the ayèn, littered throughout the different, interconnected chambers. Almost all of them had their laps filled with pretty angels, in scantily clad gowns, as they yelled at each other over tossed stones in the middle of an intense game. I search for my ayèl and found them either at the bar, minding their business as they ate their firstfast, or chatting up the courtesans who were free to talk. They were probably fishing for the latest gossip.

"Bloody cheater! Burn you in ashes, Jakran. This is the third rotting time you—"

"Rotting time I what, Ifu?" Jakran bellowed. "Skinned your rhèr, fair and square?"

I turned back to the bar and found Naveren—the owner of the *Darkwing Kiss*—glaring at my pirates. He balanced an iridescent coin purse in his palm as he grimaced. His sky-light eyes caught mine, darkening.

"You're lucky they pay well, Ashthorn."

I grinned, wriggling my brows.

"Come now, Naveren." I smiled wickedly. "How often is the *Darkwing Kiss* this lively?"

Without warning, the entire tavern abruptly fell silent. Curious, I spun around to see the reason. When my gaze fell on the troop of Airveillers, my blood ran cold.

"High Prince Yakobba Izayi Rhòdhaire, Seedling of King Izakaya Promeseren Rhòdhaire and Queen Rekani Allahiel Rhòdhaire, Uncrowned Heir to the throne of the Cloud Castle and the Avari Kingdom. You have been summoned by His Majesty and are to come with us at once."

There was an emphasis on "Uncrowned" that jabbed at my ribs with daggers.

I faced the host of Airveillers—guardians of the Cloud Castle—most of which had been my personal Airveillers since my first riseday. I found profound disappointment in their faces. Some of them regarded me with an old affection that wheedled me down to nothing but boyish shame and regal embarrassment.

All eyes in the tavern were on me. Staring. Weighing.

Unable to ignore my princely training, I bowed low. I knew I was elegant, to such a degree that even Elector Serefini, who'd been responsible for the upbringing of my courtly etiquette, would be proud. After the deep bow, I rose to face the Airveillers. Hope glittered in their pastel colored eyes as they watched me beneath ivory armor covered in luxurious lavender cloaks. Their golden halos gleamed in the mid-dawn light of the tavern.

"Airveiller Tombabi." I nodded at the herald. "You're a long way from His Majesty, King Izakaya."

Tombabi stared at me for a long time, unimpressed. He scowled at the arrogance in my voice, his dark skin mirroring his mood.

"Have you not tired of these foolish antics?" He looked around the tavern, sniffing. "Let's go, princeling. You've been summoned by the king."

"And what exactly does the king need from me?" I asked, crossing my arms. "Isn't High Prince Ishaèli home with His Majesty? Whatever the needs of the king are, surely his chosen heir, who sits on a stolen throne, is competent enough to handle it."

I began turning away when Airveiller Tombabi cleared his throat. He slammed his wings together, the sound like thunder ringing throughout the tavern. The boom reverberated through my body, throwing my limbs into momentary shock. I gasped as angels around me snarled and squealed, retreating from the Airveillers. I looked at Tombabi. His *ethèr* was swirling around him like a whirlwind.

"You will come by will," he spread his legs, wings rising behind him. "Or you will come by force." The bass of his low voice could almost be lethal. "Either way, princeling, you are coming."

I tilted my head, growing utterly still. A tense quiet made the air in the chamber brittle, ready to snap at any moment. I didn't take kindly to being told what to do. I didn't care who was calling me.

"Is that a threat, Tombabi?"

Tombabi's two-toned, light eyes flashed.

"If it needs to be, princeling." He jutted a chin to the doorway. "Are you coming? Or must we drag you?"

I pressed my lips into a flat line.

"Advise the king we make our way for him in the next wèk."

"No!" Tombabi bellowed.

Engèli snarled behind me, but did no more.

"You sail north of here now."

Then the Airveillers pressed into a tight line leading to the front door. I counted seven beats before I began floating without a backward glance.

"*Ashweaver* mates, move out!" I called.

Then I flew out of the *Darkwing Kiss*, headed for my ship, to set sail for the one place I didn't expect to see for another thousand cycles.

Home.

CHAPTER 7
SHACKLED TO SEA GRAVES
RAESHELLE

"My Pearl, will you join me in my study? I have a special task for you."

Patting my cheeks dry, I nodded at the king, leaning away from him as I worked to gather myself. The Seaveillers watched us closely, ocean-hued eyes missing nothing. They pressed in, coming closer when the king rose from the shell-chair, turning away from the bridge.

I remained where I was a beat longer, following the endless flow of life below with longing. Sea angels swam in small groups. I could tell some were with family while others were with friends. Few swam alone headed for different edifices.

I didn't know what businesses or local groups existed in the Avarien city. I'd asked the king on multiple occasions to let me frolic. Each time, he'd said no. It was too dangerous. If anything happened to me, the Rite couldn't be fulfilled, and all of Avari would be doomed.

I breathed in deep, inhaling the chilly, salty water into the thin gills on my neck and shoulders. My multi-colored, membranous wings gently flapped in the water. As water filled my lungs, I felt the rising pressure in my chest settle. If Queen Audriana could fulfill her duties to her crown, then I certainly would upkeep the responsibilities of mine.

I looked up, staring past the side of the monumental Pearl Palace, and looked at the open waters above. From my studies, I learned the Azizi kingdom was at the highest peak below the Mistwind Seas. Every other kingdom, or cluster of life, existed parallel to us, or below. The waters were dim, illuminated only by the pearls sitting inside the mouths of open clams.

"Princess Raeshelle, are you ready?"

I looked up and found payè floating several paces in front of his retinue of fearsome Seaveillers. The guards watched me with shrouded expressions. My spine tingled, but I met their gazes. Rising to a float, my feet stroked the water beneath the clinging eelsilk of my gown.

"Yes, payè, I am."

"Come."

We turned back, swimming up the sides of the Pearl Palace until we crested the open waterway that bled to the courtyard. King Bakari led the way, pivoting to the west end of the palace.

"See those high standing, colorful vines bending into an arch over there?"

I looked at where the king was pointing.

"Where there is that canopy overhang?"

"Yes, right there. Your mamè and I would take our daily dusk swims there. Once the pearls winked out and the dusk lights came on from the coral pods, she'd come to my study, take my hand, and lead us out there."

A small lump swelled into a ball in my throat. My eyes burned at the revelation. He'd never shared that before. At the tightness in his voice, I knew he was remembering her and how much he missed her.

As we swam into the palace proper, my Seaveillers joined us. Kianga, my dearest, lifelong friend, led them. She said nothing, but she gave me a small smile before falling close behind, staying near my side. My hearts calmed down, no longer racing away from an invisible threat, once Kianga drew close. I counted it strange. After all, I was with the

King of Avari, and his best, well-trained, Seaveillers. I couldn't be more safe.

Rot.

I must be tired.

I shook off the vain imaginations and followed King Bakari to the west wing of the Pearl Palace. When we entered, the foyer was dark, the water motionless. That was curious. There should be some kind of activity happening, even if it was just from a serving maydin. I grimaced at the stillness, but kept my mouth shut.

"All of you may remain here. Raeshelle and I will go to my study alone."

I bit my lip. That shouldn't have sounded as ominous as it did.

King Bakari dropped a heavy gaze on me. His pale blue and silver eyes searched me. I looked into those intelligent eyes that mirrored my own, in his wildly handsome face, and cowered. The king was tall, with broad shoulders, hardened muscles, and deep, ocean-colored hair that hung down his waist on a half-shaved head. Again, I saw why mamè couldn't resist. But as he stared at me now, I wonder how different my life would've been if she had.

"Follow me, pearling."

The king turned and swam through a set of six

ornate columns. At their center was a seventh, which stood three times wider than the rest, littered with glass murals. There were many other columns leading to different chambers. King Bakari swam to the left, his golden, sandaled feet leaving a trail of rippling bubbles behind him.

"Payè, is everything alright?" I asked, swimming ahead to join him at his side. I looked at him through my peripheral, the jewels of my gown reflecting rays of iridescent light into the chamber we swam through. "What task do you have for me to complete?"

He chuckled lightly, throwing an amused look my way.

"Truly, Raeshelle. You've got to do something about your overthinking." He tilted his head, a smile lifting his lips. "It's nothing you cannot do. I have full confidence you will get it done, and in time for El'Tide."

This had to do with the solstice? It wasn't lost on me that El'Tide this cycle would be on my riseday. The dawn all of Azizi would swim to the Atlanthyst Trench and watch me be given to the Sea in the Azizien Rite.

We flew into the king's study. I floated to one chair as he swam to sit behind his desk. There was more light here with the help of the many windows open to the sea beyond and the clam lamps with pearls inside giving off light. When King Bakari was settled in his seat, he looked at me.

"My pearling. I need you to prepare yourself." He leaned back and pulled out several capsules made of pastel crystals. Each capsule had a rolled up scroll inside with a string tied around it. I flicked my gaze from the capsules to the king, not understanding. He merely smiled as if there could be no clearer thing in all the Mistwind Seas. "You're to travel at first light."

I blinked at him.

The king's eyes were dancing.

"Travel." I repeated, tasting the foreign words on my tongue. "I rarely leave the Pearl Palace. Now you want me to travel. Where in the Sea am I to go?"

"Patience, my pearling. You're not headed somewhere in the sea. You're headed beyond the Surface. To the Cloud Castle in the sky."

My jaw hung. I had no words. I was going to the Surface? And all the way to the Avari kingdom? Was the king mad?

"You will take one of my personal sumaren to the Surface. Once you're out of water, it will convert into a chariot. You'll be flown all the way to the Cloud

Castle. I've already spoken to King Izakaya and Queen Rekani. They will be expecting you."

My knees buckled. My stomach lurched. I could sense a whopping headache coming on.

Avari.

I was going to Avari.

"Payè," I whispered. "What could you possibly need me to do in the sky kingdom?"

King Bakari Ezrathen Au'Pearl's lips curled into a smile I would almost call cruel. His eyes gloated in victory as the jaws of a trap snapped shut around me.

"The Avarien royals have been invited to El'Tide. They will also celebrate the Azizien Rite. You are to deliver their invitations. They must all be here. The king, queen, their princess, and their two princes."

Heavy stones sank in my gut. I struggled to breathe, blinking rapidly to keep from crying. My hearts constricted. This couldn't be happening. This couldn't be...

My eyes fluttered shut. The only sound I could hear was the thump, thump, thump of my racing hearts. Then I rushed out of the king's study, raced into an empty chamber, shut the door, and tumbled into a silent scream.

CHAPTER 8

ARRIVAL OF THE PIRATE PRINCE

YAKOBBA

Dropping our anchors in the Clouthren Harbor was a small mercy. We could dock and enter Avari without fanfare. I looked back at the *Ashweaver*. The crew stared with anxious expressions, their muscled arms crossed, and their wings flapping in the breeze. They looked beyond me at the Airveillers with unveiled rage. They weren't used to taking orders from anyone but me. None of them enjoyed being this close to the Avarien king's radar. They were all staying on the ship except for Engèli, Nyala, and Jabari. Jaspen, Dakri, and Ifu were none too happy about that. Ifu spat, eyes blazing at Tombabi.

Engèli, Nyala, and Jabari balanced on the cloudy ground by my side, hands on the hilt of their cutlasses. If Tombabi and his Airveillers had their way, I would be headed to the Cloud Castle alone. I snorted to myself. How naïve did they think I was?

"Stay ready so you don't have to get ready."

I looked at each of my pirates. Their frowns slowly curled into lethal grins. They each nodded, knowing exactly what I meant.

Satisfied they would stay put, I swaggered my way to the back of a kingly chariot. The vehicle was trimmed in white gold, painted like the lavender sky, crafted from the finest materials. I was almost certain mamè had ridden in this very chariot more than once.

On either side were large mechanical wings. In front of the vehicle stood seven stareagles—the giant birds with eyes like the stars and feathered coats like fresh falling snow—tall and proud. Their golden beaks and talons were resplendent. I look at the creatures and marveled.

My emotions warred inside of me, fighting for dominance. I couldn't process, couldn't handle my feelings. The opulence, the princely treatment, was all too much.

There wasn't a chance in all of Elledelle that King Izakaya had a hand in any of this. This had Queen Rekani's touch all over it. She was a lover of lavish things, and she spared no expense for her seedlings. Even if they were wayward pirates lost at sea.

Skies.

I looked at my mates. Jabari and Nyala entered the chariot, observing with quiet wonder. Nyala took in every single detail from the seats, to the windows, to the food, to the plush rugs and decorative jewels. Jabari felt the seat beneath him, unsure if what he was looking at was real.

The interior of the chariot was designed to resemble the stars. On either side of the vehicle were long and narrow protrusions covered in food, desserts, and the finest Avarien skywine. Come to think of it, this was the chariot mamè had ridden in. She'd made it her business to take me with her on trips in it in times past.

"High Prince indeed," Jabari whistled.

I turned away, flushing at his admiration, and found a stareagle staring at me. I nodded to him in respect.

"It's good to see you again, High Prince Yakobba."

His low, melodious rumble seeped into my body, washing me like rain.

"Thank you. It does my hearts a lot of good to see you, too."

The stareagle tilted his head. His eyes gleamed as if hiding a secret.

"You don't remember me, do you?"

I looked at him again. Was he different from the rest? They all looked the same. Snowy feathers, golden talons, golden beaks, and—

Skies!

On the stareagle's beak, right where his nostrils were, was a broken, jagged line of ivory. It looked like an intentional crack. But I remembered as a youngling finding a newborn stareagle, who'd tumbled from the mountains, with starlike eyes and a broken beak. We didn't think he'd survive, especially since I'd found him all alone, but I kept him and nurtured him anyway after begging the king to let me.

Wait.

Could it be?

I shot up straight, nearly slamming my head into the roof of the chariot, my vision blurring.

"Adenael?"

Engèli's eyes went wide. He would recognize that name. After all, he and I would play many games with the hatchling, for as long as mamè would allow us, when we were younglings.

The stareagle's eyes glowed, and he shook himself, starlight bursting from his coat.

"High Prince!" Adenael sang, nearly dancing on his feet. "You remember. Yes. It's me!"

My jaw hung. Engèli is sputtered in shock. Before we could say more, an Airveiller came to the side of the chariot, sealed it shut and tight, and slapped the side. Before long, the stareagles took off, and our chariot was in flight.

"He's gotten so big!" Engèli said.

I nodded, chest constricting with insufferable emotion. Skies. I missed the stareagle.

I missed home.

"He has," I rumbled. "He's grown now. Even his horns have come in. They were hidden under the feathers."

"Wow," Engèli sighed. "All that time, huh?"

I swallowed around the lump in my throat, nodding. I coughed through the tension building in my chest, focusing on the iridescent clouds as we flew through the sky.

"All that time."

The stareagles flew through Avari's vast, cloudy landscape. I watched it all go by with deepening nostalgia. There was nowhere so glorious, so majestic, as the Avari kingdom. Her glass skyscrapers, her iridescent rivers, her ivory and lavender tipped mountains, and regal Domenent angels.

I balled my hand into a fist to help guide my breathing until the stareagles landed in one of the king's courtyards, close to the royal hangar. Through the chariot window, I looked up and stared at the Cloud Castle. The ancient structure was carved of glass, crystals, and thickened clouds. Sprawled out before us, its gargantuan size took up endless miles of land. I choked on air, staring at the grandeur of it all.

My chest squeezed. Memories came rushing back without my permission. I saw myself in cycles long ago, flying through the halls, playing pranks before I became too old for such things. Then games turned into training. Training that came in handy once I began my life of pirating.

A low whistle to my left snagged my attention. Engèli said nothing, eyes glued to the place we once thought would be our future, while Jabari looked at it incredulously.

"Sheesh, Cap. This is home? Must've been bad to leave."

It was.

I didn't answer Jabari. Nyala watched me, intelligent eyes seeing more than I wished she would. She stayed quiet, but I knew she filed my silence away into the recesses of her mind.

An unceremonious knock on the side of the chariot snagged our attention. Tombabi poked his head in, glaring at Engèli, Nyala, and Jabari.

"You lot, find somewhere else to be." His elderly eyes fell on me. The weight of them made me feel small. Unworthy. "High Prince, welcome home. The king and queen await your return."

My crew looked at me, unmoving. They took orders from no one but me. If I didn't say something, they wouldn't move. I grinned, unwilling to let them see any trepidation on my face.

"I'm good. Go. Enjoy yourselves. The Shifting Shops should still be open. You've ample coin to spend. I'll find you when necessary."

They paused longer, as if they didn't trust leaving me in my home alone. I almost laughed. Eventually, they nodded, leaving the chariot and flying off.

"Come, High Prince. You must change—"

"I go as I am or I won't go at all. Then you can explain to King Izakaya, and his temper, why you've arrived empty-handed."

I brushed past Tombabi and the gaping Airveillers. Storming past the hangar, I marched to an archway on the side of the castle, walking like I owned the place. Which I did.

"Where are you—"

"I know my way around," I tossed over my shoulder. "Keep up or get left behind."

Maydins floating through the halls came to a full stop, their mouths hanging when they laid eyes on me. Wide grins covered their pretty faces as they spread their wings and took off down the hall. I stifled a groan. The castle would be full of gossip in no time.

Floating through hall after hall, I stared past foreign tapestries, endless family portraits, and numerous marble statues in fountains. I walked, taking my time, until I came to the king's wing. I stopped moving when I finally reached the door of his private dining chambers. On the other side of the door, I heard clinking glass, pleasant chatter, and soft music playing.

"Prince Yakobba, please," Tombabi pleaded. "Wait just a moment! I must announce you—"

I could announce myself.

Without ceremony, I threw the doors open and floated into the dining chambers. I stared directly at King Izakaya Promeseren Rhòdhaire, king of Avari, and my payè. There he sat at the head of the long, gilded table, mouth hanging as if he were mid-sentence. His body was angled towards Queen Rekani, while Prince Ishaèli froze, his fork midway to his mouth. Princess Alessayi, seated on the other side of the table, spat out her wine. King Izakaya's eyes landed on me like cauldrons of fire. I spread my arms wide, grinning from ear to ear.

"My dearest payè. I believe you called me?"

CHAPTER 9

INVITED TO THE DEPTHS OF THE SEA

YAKOBBA

The dining chamber was silent. Everyone was frozen in place. The Airveillers behind me shuffled quietly, unsure of how to intervene. It felt like time had slowed. I blinked at my family, all of whom I hadn't seen in nearly five cycles.

King Izakaya stiffened at the arrogance in my tone. It dawned on me that Tombabi was right. I should have changed.

The Rhòdhaires were adorned in their gilded crowns, ivory and lavender silks, golden leather sandals, and jewels embedded in their wings. Meanwhile, I was in head to toe black, my midnight cloak a stark contrast to everything else in the room. I should care.

I didn't.

"YAKOBBA!"

Princess Alessayi, six cycles my junior with twice my pompous personality, shot out of her cloudchair and flew over the table. She was low enough that her gown nearly glided through meat juice and was almost stained by the colorful desserts. Alessayi flung herself at me. Her arms were around my neck before I could stop her. My hearts felt like they'd explode as I wrapped my arms around my youngling sayè.

I chuckled into her hair. "I've missed you, too, Sayi."

She pulled back, her eyes sharp. Discerning. That look wasn't there the last time I'd seen her. She'd grown. In ways I would never know. Guilt tugged at me, but I buried it.

"Stop the nonsense," Alessayi quipped without preamble. "Come home."

"Alessayi, allow him to eat before you berate him, hm?"

I looked past my sister's hair and choked on my rising emotion.

Queen Rekani, my mamè, floated out of her chair, resplendent in beauty, grace, and power. I took her in. Her braided hair was pinned in an elegant style. The thin crown interwoven in each braid. Her hanging ivory silks that thinly veiled golden sandaled feet. I looked into her eyes and was undone. She smiled at me in the way only a mamè could. Through it, I felt her unwavering love for me pulse like heartbeats that would never cease. She looked at me with pride, with acceptance, with love, as if I had never left. The burn in my throat blocked my ability to speak.

"Queen Rekani, I..."

The words died on my tongue. I couldn't think. Couldn't move. Couldn't breathe right. Skies. I missed her so much. I'd fought it for so long. But now, floating in her presence, it was all I could do to keep from falling apart. I tried to speak, but I failed again, stumbling over each word.

"Queen Rekani, my queen, I—"

She snorted, gracefully floating over. Alessayi still hadn't let me go. Her grip tightened as mamè approached.

"Sayi, release him. It's my turn."

Alessayi rolled her eyes and reluctantly let go, but didn't float away. Before I could open my mouth again, the queen had me drawn into a hug so deep I was weakened down to my knees.

All kinds of emotions threatened to unravel me.

Queen Rekani held me close. Tight. She squeezed me like she would when I was a youngling crying in her lap after having an awful nightmare. She held me as if she didn't smell the skywine clinging to my hair. Or the fading smell of smoke clinging to my boots. As if she didn't see the fresh brands in my skin, or the worn creases at my temples.

"Mamè." I breathed in the scent of her hair. "Rot, I... mamè."

I hung on to her as if I'd been thirsty a long time and was finally drinking water. Tears streamed down my cheeks, unbidden. I tried to restrain myself, but I couldn't. Not with her. Not held in her arms like this.

"It's good to have you back home, my soè."

I didn't answer. I couldn't. Burying my face in her shoulder, it took a moment to pick out the snort that hung in the air. The bitterness spoiling the sweet moment, demanding to be seen. Heard. Felt.

"The prodigal rotpot returns. He's shamed this castle, this kingdom, our name, and this is the greeting he receives?"

An icy rage, with cycles of fuel, churned in my gut. My wrath flared, howling for release. I vowed to not lose control and box Ishaèli upside his head, but it was a hard vow to keep the longer he talked.

"He belongs in the dungeon." Ishaèli sucked his teeth. "He actually belongs in the Saelus Prison for committing high treason. I don't even understand why he's here. Looking like a savage vagabond coughed up by the—"

"Silence, Ishaèli!"

The king's harsh rebuke was cutting, even to my ears.

I snapped my head up, meeting his swirling light eyes. The king was not happy to have me home. He looked at me in the queen's embrace, his frown deepening, his disappointment clear. A cold shiver snaked down my spine. I hadn't even done anything yet. Still, he was ready to be rid of me. I longed to embrace him like mamè, but I knew that was a dream for fools.

Mamè released me and nudged me forward.

Ignoring Ishaèli's existence, I floated over to King Izakaya. I lowered myself into a bow befitting a king, then rose enough to reach forward and leave a gentle kiss on his signet ring. When I pulled back, his eyes were bristling. I couldn't make out the expression on his hardened, earthen face.

"Yakobba Izayi," the king breathed. My name hung in the air. I waited for a lashing, for rebuke, for something of major consequence. "You haven't changed."

My eyes flicked down to his. I plastered an affable grin on my face, refusing to cower, even if my hearts were racing inside of me.

"I'm too old to change."

"Is that so, Izayi?"

The king looked at me, his expression guarded. It took everything in me to not fidget. I stood tall, proud, with my shoulders squared and chin lifted. King Izakaya looked on, stroking his bearded chin. The agelessness of angels made him look only a few cycles my senior. But payè had seen at least three millethium and had ruled for two of them.

"You came," he says after a while. "Good. I received word from the Azizi king, King Bakari Ezra-then Au'Pearl. His dayè is on her way now with an official invitation from the Azizien king. I need you here when she arrives."

I blinked at the king, confused. He couldn't have possibly made me travel all this way just for some invitation. Besides, what business did we have with the sea kingdom? In my cycles at sea, I hadn't once come across sea dwelling angels. So why were we engaging now?

"Sit down, Yakobba."

"Payè, I'm not staying long. My crew is waiting for me. I'm sure this invitation—"

"I said sit down."

King Izakaya's eyes flashed, commanding obedience. I looked around. There was one seat left. A seat on the king's right side. The seat of power. The seat of authority.

The seat of the king's heir.

I flickered my gaze to Ishaèli. We had the same face and height. Where he had lighter features, I had darker ones. Where I had blackened hair like mamè, he had silver hair like payè. I was lean but wiry. He was wide and all muscle. Outside of that, we were practically the same.

I sat down at the king's right hand, which effectively sat me between payè and Ishaèli.

Queen Rekani and Princess Alessayi returned to their seats, eyes glued to me. King Izakaya continued speaking, without looking at me, as he began adding more food to his plate.

"The Aziziens will soon celebrate El'Tide. It is their solstice where they celebrate the glory of their kingdom. All angels, including commoners, are invited to the Pearl Palace to feast, then they travel to the Atlanthyst Trench and perform a final ritual. We have all been invited. There is something special happening this cycle and King Au'Pearl wants to build relations between our kingdoms by inviting us of Avari to witness it."

"What does any of this have to do with—"

"Surely living like some imbecile pirate hasn't made you daft." The king glared at me from the corner of his eye, silencing my next words. "You will be here for the invitation, and you will attend El'Tide. That is final, Yakobba." He watched me, exasperated. "I fetched you from this nonsense living so you'd be aware. You will go. And if you don't, I'll have that rotting ship torched and burned." A pause. "With your crew still on it."

He leveled a hard gaze at me that made my blood run cold.

"You are a Rhòdhaire, and still the heir to the throne. You will attend as such. The matter is decided. Now, eat. Your mamè had all of your favorites prepared."

With that, King Izakaya turned to add more meats and cheeses to his plate while I sat glued to my chair, ridiculed by my unseen crown.

CHAPTER 10
FROM THE SEA TO THE SKIES
RAESHELLE

I am both grateful and unimpressed as we journey to the Surface.

"I expected this to be a... longer trip," I told Kianga. She's seated at my right, her legs crossed, as she idly plays with one of her wings. Her trident is balanced on her hip, bouncing as the sumaren travels along. "More complicated, even."

My Seaveiller turned to me, her ocean blue and fiery orange eyes shining. She gave me a pretty smile. Too pretty for a Seaveiller, but I kept the thought to myself. Her tiny scales shimmered under the growing light of the sôlight above, beaming through the Surface of the Mistwind Sea.

"My guess is, we're using uncommon waterways," Kianga said. "I overheard King Bakari, long may he reign, telling Wheel Ryder Tunde to make sure we moved with the speed of sea serpents. I think the Avariens are expecting us in no less than a few dawns."

My eyebrows arched like reefs balanced atop hidden sea coves. A few dawns? Was payè mad?

"But Kia, how could he assume we could cross so much sea in such little time?"

Kianga shrugged. "Beats me."

"I think it's because the king has gone to the Surface himself," Tobe butted in. His mauve and emerald eyes danced between the eight Wheel Ryders, navigating the sumaren at a speed that made the fastest shrarks look like seaslugs.

Tobe looked uncomfortable, his face contorting into a grimace. I didn't blame him. Traveling this fast had to be illegal. But if the king had given his permission...

"I think we are using a waterway no one in either kingdom knows about. There's barely any fish out here. And no chance of Serène, Maergels, or Troks, either. We can move."

I snorted. "We're moving alright."

The weight of the invitation I carry didn't help my mood. I wanted to throw the thing in a frost spring, watch it turn to a block of ice, and explode.

The Seaveillers, all from my personal guard, had their eyes on the water. Everything was a blur. I couldn't make note of the changes to the Mistwind Seas here. We were going too fast. My hearts pound in my chest. I did not want to go to the sky kingdom. There wasn't a single good thing that could come from me going to Avari. Not one.

"Don't try to look like the dead so soon," Terfitti quipped.

We all snapped our gazes at her. I hissed at the insult, wanting to shred her gills and block her waterflow.

"Excuse you?" I said in a low voice. "How dare you suggest—"

"The truth, princess?" Terfitti lifted her chin, squaring her shoulders. She was tall, so I had to look up to glare at her. "We all know El'Tide is soon. The time has come, Princess Raeshelle. Quit moping. We all have duties. You do, too."

I lift a hand, silencing whatever she planned to say next.

"That's enough, Seaveiller."

The other Seaveillers glared at Terfitti, several scrunching their nose with disgust and anger. Kianga looked at her with downright hatred. I knew the two didn't get along. Being this close to Terfitti, I could understand why.

The sumaren fell silent and remained that way for the next four dawns. We got closer and closer to approaching the Surface. Ignoring everything but the capsule in my possession, I kept my eyes on the dividing line between sea and sky. It was terrifying knowing I would soon be out of the sea. I'd never even left the kingdom. Leaving Mistwind altogether had me shaken to my core. All because payè wanted the Avariens at El'Tide, in the name of building relations between the kingdoms. A barrel full of searot is what it all was.

I brushed the skirts of my gown, feeling the large lump in my throat swell. All I want to do was curl up into a ball and cry. I stared off into nothing, awaiting the beginning of my end.

As the sumaren pressed towards the Surface, I noticed traces of the Taint. There were streaks of oily darkness in the water that could only mean one thing. Poison. None of us knew where the Taint came from. All that was clear was, everywhere there was the Taint, all sea life died.

That would explain why there was no life here. No fish, no angels, no corals, nothing.

It shocked me to see how bad the Taint was beyond Azizien waters.

How long had the waters here been like this?

I groaned, getting it. If I didn't give my life, this would just get worse. These waters wouldn't ever heal. I could plainly see all the reasons I had to fulfill the Azizien Rite, but it didn't make the decision any easier.

"Surface ahead!" Wheel Ryder Tunde shouted. The sumaren bustled into life. "Etheriscs on!"

Kianga came to my side to help me put my etherisc on. She opened her palm. At its center, a star-shaped clip floated. The instrument was small, seemingly insignificant, but I was not so naïve. Without it I wouldn't be able to breathe above the Surface, or walk like the sky angels, and my body would die leaving my spirit in a hellish limbo.

"Here goes," I mumbled to myself. "The beginning of the end."

Kianga laughed softly beside me. "Stop it. Nothing is ending. I don't know how yet, but I have a gut feeling. Things won't go as you think. Besides," she shrugged. "I'm too stubborn. I'm not losing my best friend that easily. We have a millethium of world and life to see. Together."

I smiled and gave her a hug. We held each other

a moment, bracing ourselves for the unexpected, before letting go.

"I'll attach the etherisc to the top of your spinal column between your wings. The ethereal substance should emit throughout your wings and body. Everything else should take care of itself after that."

I nodded in understanding. Kianga turned me around, clipping the etherisc to the spinal column of my wings. A strange sensation, like warm water melting ice, washed me from my tiara to my sandaled feet. As the sensation passed, I craved something I'd never had before. I breathed in, desperate for...

"Air," Kianga whispered. "I hope Tunde didn't have us put them on too soon. We need air or else..." she trailed off.

I tried not to fidget. Not to breathe too much.

My chest burned, the sensation only growing. I fought to be still, but I could feel myself twitching. Feel myself about to combust. My chest tightened. I felt like I was caving inward. Felt like I was dying when—

The sumaren bursted through the Surface of the Mistwind Seas.

Wheel Ryder Tunde began pushing buttons on his dashboard. In a blink, the vessel morphed from a sumaren to a king-sized chariot with wings. The moment I felt a light breeze on my neck, I tilted my head back, and... breathed. I drank in the thin, cool air, satisfying my lungs.

"Aziziens," Tunde called. "We've reached the Surface. And right above, a little ways away, there lies the kingdom of Avari."

CHAPTER 11

PLANTING SEEDS

YAKOBBA

When rays of sôlight reflected in my chambers through closed blinds, I threw off my duvet and rolled out of my bedcloud. Incessant chatter flittered into my bedchamber as maydins dashed back and forth preparing for the sea princess. I ignored it, heading for my bathing rooms. The bath was glorious, and I indulged myself staying longer than I needed to. While the castle was busy welcoming the princess of Azizi, I planned to be long gone.

Payè was adamant during supprèst. Every Rhòd-haire had to be present for her arrival. This Azizi invitation was a big deal. One payè planned to drain of all its benefits. When I asked questions, he dodged them while Ishaèli was showered with his attention and pride. Mamè and Alessayi were the ones to remind me I still belonged inside the castle. As always.

Looking at myself in a long mirror, I appraised my attire. I dressed in head to toe black, covered in my floor length leather cloak. I smiled. Payè had another thing coming. Every Rhòdhaire would be present.

Every Rhòdhaire but me.

I hadn't fully decided on where to go just yet, but I was well accustomed to getting lost.

I floated over to my scrollshelf, pulled a scroll-book forward, and watched a doorway form. I floated through and let the secret doorway fall shut with a click.

The stones of the secret passage were freshly polished. The floors were paved smooth. Ishaèli and I had stumbled on these passages accidentally when we were younglings while running from our Electors. From then on, we used them to pull pranks on the king and queen, but especially Alessayi. When we got older, we'd sneak in and out of the castle, bringing inappropriate company, as mamè labeled it.

I recalled those dawns with profound sadness. Those dawns were long gone. Ishaèli outgrew those cycles, and me. He became the favorite of payè while I was mamè's. I always wondered why I was chosen as heir and not Ishaèli, but refused to learn the truth.

I floated along through the corridors without aim until I found myself balanced behind a protruding stone. Pushing it down, I floated into the chamber it led to. I looked around for two beats before I cursed and rushed back into the secret corridor.

"Soè."

Mamè's cool voice called to me from deep inside her chambers. I silently cursed myself for not being able to piece together where I was sooner.

"Izayi, come."

Unbidden, I felt my body moving, as if pulled on an invisible chain. I floated back in and found Queen Rekani perched on a floating couch of gilded clouds, sipping on a mug of tea. Mamè patted the seat beside her, still sipping as if she hadn't been interrupted. I shuffled over, tucking my wings close.

"I am not your payè, Izayi." Her eyes found me above the ring of her mug. "Free your wings."

I loosed a tight breath, releasing my wings. I flexed them wide, so they hung loose behind the cloudchair, sprawled all over mamè's rugs.

"You've grown. But not so much. The stubbornness hasn't left your jawline yet," she mused, eyeing me from the corner of her eye.

This dawn, her wavy hair was worn loose, tumbling past her hips, pooling onto the couch. She looked like a youngling straight from her primary cycles. Everything about her was ageless, except for her shrewd eyes. I chuckled at her observation and look her in the eyes, feeling safe, and wholly loved.

"I miss you often while at sea."

"Yet you don't call me or write to me."

She watched me in amusement as I fidgeted beneath that gaze that saw more than she'd ever tell. I opted not to say anything. The sea princess crossed my mind, and I nearly jumped out of my seat.

"Mamè, what are you doing here? You should be headed for the throne room."

Queen Rekani smiled. I shrank at the knowing in her eyes. Skies. Why did it feel like she was always thirty steps ahead?

"I could say the same for you, Izayi."

"I'll be there soon enough." The lie tasted like ash on my tongue.

Queen Rekani snorted, laughing into her mug.

"I carried you for what felt like ten long cycles." Her eyes flashed. "The way you nearly destroyed my knees and back... it's a wonder I could ever properly fly again." A pause. "Do you think me a fool, Izayi?" She shook her head. "Just keep whatever it is you're up to quiet." She looked at me. "You better think of a good excuse to appease your payè. I can't bail you out of this one. Not this time."

My jaw hung. How did she...

"Mamè, I—"

She waved a hand, dismissing me.

"Your payè wants something, Yakobba."

Her eyes glittered with mischief. The same kind that always had me pissing off Ishaèli and getting into trouble with the king. Skies. What was she up to?

"He wants it bad." She paused, sipping her tea, before continuing. "You're the only one I know who can retrieve it."

"Mamè..." I drawled.

What could the king possibly want that he couldn't get for himself? That not even Ishaèli could get for him?

"You're a... pirate. No?"

I frowned. "Yes..."

"Good. Your skills are needed." Her eyes flickered to me above the rim of her mug. "Your payè wants the stone."

My blood ran cold. There was only one stone in the entire realm of Zurethe a king could want so badly.

"Which stone?"

"The Atlanthyst Stone. And it's located in the Pearl Palace."

Bollocks! I knew it. I hissed, throwing my head back as I wrang my fingers through my hair.

"Mamè!"

I struggled to breathe. She couldn't be serious.

She wanted me to steal the Atlanthyst Stone out of the Pearl Palace? It was said the Atlanthyst Stone was the reason for Azizi's incontestable power. It was the salvation of the kingdom from another realm, delivered by angels of Saerel rank. No one outside of the sea could possess the stone without being ruined.

"You're always simpering for your payè's affections. Well?" She looked at me, eyes gleaming in pride, her trap well set. "You've got your chance. Take it."

With that, she shot to her feet, brushed the length of her regal skirts, and patted her hair into place. Straightening her crown, she looked at me fondly and left a gentle kiss on my forehead before floating away.

"If you make a mess before you leave, tidy it up," she tossed over her shoulder. With that, she's gone.

I fell back onto the couch, jaw still working wrong.

The Atlanthyst Stone!

Bloody skies.

Was mamè trying to get me killed? But she was right. I'd been trying to win payè's approval my entire life. If he wanted the stone, and I was the only one who could get it for him...

A grin slowly spread across my face. I flew off the couch and back into the secret passageways, leaving mamè's chamber as tidy as I found it. It didn't take me long to find the stone that would lead to the chamber I'd bargained for Engèli to stay in. When I barged in, he was still lounging in bed with a pretty ayèl, her nude body curled under his.

"Engèli, get up."

Engèli shot out of the bedcloud, cutlass already in hand, *ethèr* winding around the blade. When he saw it was me, his eyes were flames of fire.

"What in the hells—"

"Get dressed."

I grinned as Engèli blinked away sleep.

"Gather the crew. I have a job for us."

CHAPTER 12
WHEN SEA MEETS SKY
RAESHELLE

I looked out at the Avari kingdom in pure wonder. Never in all my dawns had I seen anything like it. Pressed against the floor to roof windows of the chariot, I gaped at this kingdom in the sky.

"Their ground is... clouds," Kianga whispered from somewhere beside me.

"Screw the ground. Do you see what they're wearing? All those rotting layers?"

Sniggers filled the chariot at Matteyo's outburst. Jenessa jumped in, agreeing with him.

"Matteyo has a serious point. All those layers would be insufferable under the sea. We could never."

Terfitti grunted but says nothing. She's kept quiet

since the dawn she rudely pointed out I was on a fast track to entering the Ellelights.

"I think it's all glorious," I said wistfully. "Look at their iridescent halos. Can you imagine what those lavender silks must feel like?" I point to a cluster of magnificent towers carved of glass that reflect the lavender sky. "And those buildings there? They look like shops or something similar. I'd love to get lost in there."

"Mhm," Kianga agreed. "And look at their ayèn."

Jenessa whistled. "They're soft on the eyes, for sure."

"Shame they need air to breathe," Kianga grumbled.

"A well-crafted etherisc can fix anything," Jenessa suggested. "I see no reason we can't bring a few of them home."

I whipped around to look at Jenessa, wide-eyed.

"Is your brain broken? They're not toys. You can't just take them off the street and bring them under the sea."

"Why not?" Jenessa asked, tilting her head. "They look like toys. Perhaps they'll be equally fun."

Jenessa wriggled her brows suggestively. My jaw hung. I'd always known the Seaveiller was more promiscuous than I could stomach, but rot. She couldn't be serious.

"No."

Jenessa pouted, then shrugged. "Fine."

"Anyway, they're so different," Tobe commented.

"How?" Zukon added in, finally joining the conversation for the first time this entire trip. The honey eyed angel was as large as he was reserved. He only spoke when necessary, always watching but never speaking. Still, he was a consistent, calm presence. "They can't be all that different. They're Domenents, just like us."

"Being from the same angelic rank means absolutely nothing," Tobe retorted. "We're Domenents of the sea. These angels know nothing of the worlds below the Surface."

"True," I jumped in. "But we know nothing of the sky, either. I mean, can you even walk?"

Kianga snorted, then bent over and busted out laughing. Jenessa joined her, sliding out of her seat, laughing with her entire body.

Zukon's eyes widened, his nostrils flaring, as his handsome face split into a grin. "Princess, that's foul."

"How?" I threw my hands up. "That's a serious question. I can walk because I was taught. I thought the lessons were a waste of time, but now I'm grateful. Can the rest of you?" I looked at Tobe through a side glance. "Can't keep doing a lot of talking if you can't even do the basics."

"Sheesh," Zukon coughed, barking out a laugh. "Raeshelle, two. Tobe, zero."

The Wheel Ryders chuckled at the front of the chariot as they pivoted the vehicle across the Avarien skies. I memorized as much as I could of the rivers and mountains. I looked at the sky beasts and the clusters of neighborhoods. There had to be countless millions of angels in the entire kingdom.

The sight overwhelmed me. I was lost in taking it all in, hardly listening to the mindless chatter behind me, until we neared the enormous castle of glass and crystal shrouded in iridescent clouds.

"Burning seas," Kianga whispered. "I thought the Pearl Palace was huge. The Cloud Castle could give us a run for our seashells."

"That's an understatement," Jenessa breathed. "Sheesh."

Panic settled in the core of my gut, but I buried it. Terrified or not, I had a job to do. I thought of the capsule and felt myself getting sick. Kianga placed a gentle hand on my arm.

"I'm right behind you." I looked at her, knowing my fear was clear as dawn on my face. "Always."

"Thanks, Kia."

I took a deep breath and steeled myself as Tunde and his Wheel Ryders began bringing the chariot to a descent at the front of the Cloud Castle. The moment we landed, my Seaveillers and the entire Azizien retinue accompanying me launched into action, quickly dismounting the chariot.

In front of the Cloud Castle, several rows of Sky Watchers and Airveillers floated in perfect lines, chins lifted in Avarien pride. Armored in white with lavender and golden details, I couldn't help but feel intimidated. It wasn't until I saw my Seaveillers stepping out onto the cloudy ground with Azizien confidence that I felt better. Avari may be a force in the skies, but Azizi reigned the seas. With that reminder to myself, I shuffled past the commotion on the chariot, and exited with a regality that would make King Bakari, and the entire Azizien kingdom, proud.

I walked with grace, with elegance, head held high, as I glided to the front of my procession. When I stopped, the entire Avarien retinue bowed. When they rose again, the Airveiller leading their force greeted me from across the cloudy lawn.

"Princess Raeshelle Corellis Au'Pearl, Dayè of His

Majesty, King Bakari Ezrathen Au'Pearl, Pearl of the Mistwind Seas, we of Avari, angels of His Majesty, King Izakaya Promeseren Rhòdhaire, welcome you to our kingdom."

I curtsied low and rose, bowing my head at this Airveiller.

"It is my honor to be with you and the Avarien kingdom on behalf of my payè, King Bakari Au'Pearl of Azizi. Thank you for the gracious welcome. I look forward to meeting His Majesty and Ayella, King Izakaya and Queen Rekani Rhòdhaire. Shall we?"

The Airveiller smiled warmly, his two-toned light eyes beaming brightly. I fought not to fidget under the insufferable heat that was beating down on my temples. It felt like I'd been shoved into an oven full of hot coals. I took deep breaths, trying for the life of me to cool down.

The Airveillers, followed by the Sky Watchers, turned and began floating into the Cloud Castle. I follow on foot, refusing to embarrass myself by trying to fly without having practiced the act yet. It was one thing to use my wings below the sea, and something else entirely to fly in the sky.

Waltzing into the Cloud Castle, I was pleased with the luxury and decor, but not impressed. Admittedly, payè had much the same taste as these

Avarien royals. From the tapestries, to the marbled statues, if colors were changed and materials mixed, everything in the Cloud Castle was much the same as the Pearl Palace.

Finally, we reached the throne room. The Airveiller ushered me inside before the Avarien royals. I busied myself with analyzing these rulers of the sky. King Izakaya and Queen Rekani Rhòdhaire were resplendent. Blessed searot. They had the faces of gods. The profundity of their beauty left me speechless and squirming in place.

"Princess Raeshelle, what an honor."

King Izakaya's smile chilled me to my toes. An ayèn of his age and prominence should never be allowed to look at a youngling, dim-witted princess like that. I felt myself flushing at his keen, watchful stare. I curtsied low before the king.

"Thank you, King Izakaya. The honor truly is mine."

I turned to Queen Rekani and greeted her with the same reverence. The queen left the king's side, rushing forward to embrace me. I held her, squeezing her with the same excitement. My hearts were beating in my chest but I smiled sweetly despite it all.

"Princess Raeshelle," Queen Rekani cooed, her

eyes glittering with glee. "Welcome to our home, darling. It is so good to have you. You're as I expected. As beautiful as all of Azizi."

I blushed. Before I could answer, the queen's embrace was replaced by that of the chatty princess. Princess Alessayi spoke so much, so fast. All I could do was smile and nod.

We go through the pleasantries of royals before I pulled out the capsules and officially offered them to King Izakaya. I kept my smile on my face, but inside I was dying.

The king said something, but I didn't hear it. A crack split my chest, causing a gaping hole within me. I felt a rush of tears daring to spill in front of the Rhòdhaire's as they chattered excitedly about El'Tide. I would not cry.

I would not cry.

Not here.

Not now.

I completely disassociated from the moment, turning it all off, going through motions I prayed I never remembered, until a thought crystalized in my mind, the fleeting thing sharp and jarring.

"King Rhòdhaire," I blurted out.

King Izakaya blinked at me, waiting for me to continue.

"Have you not two princes?"

I gestured to the brooding prince floating behind the queen and princess. His inquisitive eyes analyzed me like I was a piece of freshly skinned fish. His handsome face contorted into a sneer, his eyes flashing at my observation.

"I see one. Where is the other?"

The king's lips pressed into a thin line.

"Payè instructed me to be sure you would all be present."

"I have two princes. I can assure both High Prince Ishaèli and High Prince Yakobba will be present for El'Tide."

Yakobba.

The name rang in my mind, already taking root. I wanted to meet the prince with the gall to skip my arrival. Who was he? And why did the sound of his name twist my hearts with desire?

CHAPTER 13

TO ROB THE SEAS

YAKOBBA

"This better be rotting good, Ashthorn."

Nyala ground her teeth. She looked ready to skin me alive. She sat across from me in the booth, arms crossed, wings twitching in agitation.

"It was time for you to wake up," I waved her away with a fork. "Stop whining." I wiped my mouth and took a swig of skywine before looking at my mates.

"I have a job for you."

Their eyes sparkled as each one sat straight, looking at me expectantly.

I peaked around *The Crowned Bastard*. I couldn't have anyone eavesdropping. With a measure of *ethèr*, I formed a cloudy barrier around our booth. Invisible, but thick. While we could see everything going on in the tavern, no one could hear or see us. For all they would know, it would seem as if this booth was empty.

"I was with Mamè just now."

"How is the queen?" Engèli asked.

"Very good, actually." I smiled, thinking of her. "She's aging backwards. Still sees me as a youngling, too. I don't think that'll ever change."

Engèli chuckled. Growing up around Ishaèli and I, before flying off to train as an El'Guard, he'd had his share of her motherly ways.

"Mamè always had sharp ears. Better than maydins, even."

"I take it she's heard something of importance?" Nyala asked, quirking a brow.

I leaned forward, waving my fork with a poached egg on it.

"King Izakaya wants something only a crew of lawless pirates can get for him."

I wriggled my brows before shoving the eggs into my mouth.

"Something exists that King Rhòdhaire can't get himself?" Jabari sputtered, his own mouth full of sausages and potatoes. "And what would that be?"

"The Atlanthyst Stone."

Engèli spat out his kakonut cider, choking on the strong, sparkling drink caught in his throat. Nyala's eyes widened, and she flexed her small hands. Jabari's mouth hung open. The three blinked at me, not comprehending. Then they spoke all at once.

"Of all the bloody gems, he wants the Atlanthyst Stone?" Jabari cried.

"Isn't that stone buried deep in the Pearl Palace?" Nyala seethed.

"King Izakaya has never been above causing chaos, but this?" Engèli blubbered.

"Are all of you done?" I blinked, waiting patiently. "Because we're going for the stone. I've already decided."

"Captain, be serious," Nyala snapped. "How in the rot are we supposed to get into the Pearl Palace and steal the stone?"

"I have a plan."

Jabari groaned, loosing a small, chortling cry as Nyala looked like she wanted to burn down *The Crowned Bastard*, with me in it.

"I have a plan, he says. He always has a plan," Nyala snarled.

I wriggled my brows again.

"Stop the nonsense, all of you. We have plans to

make. And fast. We need to get to Azizi before the princess returns home."

"How exactly are we supposed to do that? Even if we get to Azizi, how would we get into the palace?" Engèli, asked.

"Easy," I grinned. "We have invitations. King Bakari invited the entire Rhòdhaire house to celebrate Azizi's El'Tide. Their solstice happens in thirty dawns. We need to get there in twenty."

Engèli nodded, his eyes distant, already planning on how to get in and out of the sea kingdom.

"We can do it," Nyala said. "But we have to be precise. Any missteps and we're dead."

I agreed, taking another bite of eggs and roasted potatoes.

"I figure all we need is us." I talked as I chewed. "Gèli will get us there and double as muscle. Might have to take out a Seaveiller, or two."

Engèli chuckled before diving back into his plate.

"Bari can be our go-between or..." I paused. Jabari lifted his eyes, curiosity clouding his irises. "A distraction if needed."

Jabari choked on his cider. "Rotting no—"

"Nya can learn everything about the palace. Ins, outs, all of that."

Nyala nodded, her mind already plotting.

"And..." I paused, again. They looked at me, waiting. "We'll also need Aisha."

Nyala practically flipped the table, shooting out of her seat, slamming her wings together. Jabari choked on his food, fists flexing, while Engèli snarled like a mountain baere, ready to fight.

"Her brain is bigger than Avari and Azizi combined," I cried out. "She has connections down there and without her perfect memory of all the waterways, we won't make it to Azizi. We need her."

"She's a sellout," Nyala hissed, eyes flashing.

"That's a bit far, don't you think?"

Nyala sucked her teeth long. "One of these dawns, you'll listen to me. I promise you, you will."

"It'll be fine. What we need now is to nail how to do it. Stealing the stone and sneaking out alive... I haven't gotten that far yet. All of my ideas end one way." I blinked at them. "With all of us dead."

"Bully a sea angel to help us?" Jabari suggested.

"No," we all answered collectively.

"Go in disguised, find it, leave with it."

"And the moment Aziziens learn of its absence, their hunt will begin," I countered. "So, no."

"Break in with a *monseriö*, reign down mayhem, nab it in the chaos, and swim off?"

"Really, Jabari, just shut up," Nyala rolled her eyes.

"We create a duplicate."

We all fell silent, blinking at Engèli. He shrugged, cheeks flushing, eyes on his plate as he pushed his food around.

"Aisha..." He stumbled on her name. "Aisha can learn exactly what it looks like. Bari and I can find what we need to create it. Nya can make it. We set sail, enter as your guests, use some kind of diversion, swap at out the stones, and as the Aziziens party, we get the rot out of there."

"Well, I'll be rotting burned," Nyala smiled prettily, making Engèli blush.

"I have more than just marbles for brains, you know," Engèli says, sheepishly, his enormous hands slapping more food onto his plate.

"Rot, Gèli. You've nailed it," I beamed.

Engèli lifted his chin in pride.

I thought of what it would be like to find the stone. Hold it. Bring it to payè. He would be so proud of me. He'd...

I shook off the emotions. My need for payè's affections was intoxicating. If I got the stone for him, I would never compete with Ishaèli again.

I took a deep breath, reined myself in, and put on

my easy flare, as if nothing happened. I looked around and found Engèli watching me.

He saw.

He always did.

I looked away. The cloudy barrier rippled. Then a courtesan popped her head into our booth.

"High Prince Ya—"

"Say your peace or I'll have you hanged."

Instantly, her smile disappeared.

"I said I was not to be disturbed. One—"

"A message for you comes from King Izakaya!"

The courtesan thrusted an astroproge into the center of the booth. An image surfaced from the oval device of cloud and smoke displaying the king in his private chambers. The image had perfect detail, as if we were in his chambers with him.

King Rhòdhaire only had eyes for me.

"Yakobba Izayi Rhòdhaire, I swear it! Your head will be on a pike once these rotting El'Tide festivities are done. I told you to be here for the arrival of the princess. You deliberately disobeyed me!"

King Izakaya was fuming. Everyone in the booth was looking everywhere but at me.

"May the first part of your punishment begin. You're to accompany part of her retinue on that accursed ship back to Azizi. This will ensure your arrival and your presence. If you dare to disgrace my crown by being absent during El'Tide, Yakobba, I swear." The king heaved, trying, and failing, to calm himself. I twitched in my seat, terrified he'd jump out of the astroproge and beat me where I sat. "If I have to unleash every Sky Watcher in all of Avari to hunt you down and return you to me, I will. And I promise you, when I am through, you will have wished for a lifetime in the dungeons with only a pot to piss in."

Jabari whistled low, his ears twitching.

"Are you done threatening my soè?" Queen Rekani asked in a husky voice. "Leave him be, Iza. He will be there. He has to be." Her voice held a knowing. "Now end this. You've given enough attention to everyone else. It's my turn."

Then the astroproge winked out.

Nyala's sour face could curdle milk.

"If we bring sea angels, and they find out—"

"They won't." I drank a goblet of skywine in one go. "After all, it's Mistwind." I winked at her. "Accidents happen all the time."

Engèli chuckled darkly. Jabari smiled, a similar glint in his eyes. Nyala shrugged, waving her fork as if to call us idiots.

"Now." I rubbed my hands. "Ready to begin?"

CHAPTER 14
CAUGHT IN THE MIDDLE
RAESHELLE

"Raeshelle, this is so dumb."

Kianga trailed me through the corridors of the Cloud Castle. Scooting along, hot irritation tensed my shoulders. I was completely out of my element here. I had to walk when I wanted to swim. Breathe through my nose instead of my neck. Everywhere I went, sky angels stared. It was all I could do to keep from going mad.

"If it's so dumb, go back to the Seaveillers. I didn't ask you to come."

"You can cop an attitude, but that won't change the fact that this is dumb," Kianga snapped back.

I ignored her, turning a corner and stomping down another long, insufferable hall. These Rhòdhaires were good at showing off. Every detail of this castle screamed wealth. None of it impressed me.

I focused on my feet, praying I wouldn't trip. Again. Every hallway we walked was covered in carpet. I was sick of it. Why couldn't this rubbish castle have marbled floors throughout? I lost my sense of balance on the carpet and my knees buckled. I caught myself just in time before I fell.

"Bloody carpets," I mumbled, brushing the length of my skirts before marching on.

"Raeshelle," Kianga snapped, again. "We will get caught."

"Is that supposed to mean something to me?" I tossed over my shoulder. "I told you I'm not leaving before I find him."

Castle gossip would serve me well this dawn. I'd overheard the maydins saying they spotted the dust licking prince at some depraved tavern called *The Crowned Bastard*. I blushed at the name. It was crass and inappropriate. All I had to do was leave the castle through the gardens, slip into a side street paved with lavender stones, and fly until I reached the gilded doors. Then, I needed to say the magic words, and I'd be allowed in. I stomped on, determined to find the karraba eating prince and give him a piece of my mind.

"This is dangerous," Kianga said. "You heard the maydins. He's more pirate than prince. You don't know how he'll react. What if you don't survive the encounter?"

I said nothing. I'd thought about it. But nothing could match my fury at his utter disregard. His lack of appearance wasn't just dishonorable to me. He'd disgraced our entire kingdom. He was the crowned heir of Avari, and by choosing not to be present, he effectively said Azizi could kiss his rhèr because we weren't worth his time.

I flared with indignation. That good-for-nothing balls for brains was about to learn something new this dawn.

We scurried out of the side door that led to one of the gardens. I prayed it would take me to the side street leading to *The Crowned Bastard.* When I stepped outside, Avarien air rammed into me like a heated hammer. Searot. It was blazing hot! I fanned my face, growing even more irritable, as my scales grew hot as fire. I noticed Kianga struggling with the heat, too. How the Avariens managed this hellish existence each dawn was beyond either of us. I took another step and ran into my retinue of Seaveillers.

"Rot," I grumbled.

"We can't let you leave, Princess Raeshelle."

Getting past Terfitti was going to be a special kind of hells. My Seaveillers stood behind her, hands on their tridents as if prepared for battle. I bit my lip. I had to get to that tavern.

"Terfitti, step aside. I am going."

Terfitti squared her jaw, spreading her stance. The stubborn headed shell eater.

"We have strict orders from King Au'Pearl—"

"Payè wouldn't have agreed to you shackling me like some Condemned," I snapped. "Terfitti, move."

Kianga whistled low. "I told you to leave this to me, but you never listen."

Terfitti snarled, lifting her chin.

"Enough," I stomped a foot. "Get out of my way. Stop me and your heads will be on tridents when we get home."

Scurrying past them as they stood in the gardens with their jaws hanging, I stumbled out onto a side street and turned down the walkway with lavender stones. I trailed them until I found the gilded door. I knocked twice.

"Password."

"I am a bastard."

A grunt and shuffle sounded, then the door swung wide. A burly angel filled the doorway with a petite angel hanging on his arm. I flushed, guessing what they'd been up to.

"So the sea princess wants some Avarien fun, huh?"

I knew enough to not give my identity away lest I draw too much attention.

"If you think I'm the princess, you're as daft as you look." I lifted my chin, eyes burning into his. His smile wavered. "I am an Ayella-in-waiting, an attendant of our princess. Surely you know more of Azizi than this?"

He blinked. Before I could be caught on my bluff, I spoke again.

"Will you let me in or not?"

"Come in, seastress."

The angel grinned, but I ignored him and the heat flaming my cheeks at the scandalous title. I brushed past him and looked around. *The Crowned Bastard* was larger than I expected. The foyer bled into side rooms while a wide ramp led upstairs.

"Where is the prince? Yakobba, to be clear. Not Ishaèli."

"Almost every pretty little thing like you comes for the unwanted prince whose shaved rhèr sits wrongfully on our throne. Few have the gall to come for the bastard one." He wriggled his brows. "Follow the columns to the back and you'll find him." He paused. "Hopefully alone. That one is a rascal who likes his fun."

The burly angel winked and turned back to the angel still clinging to him. The moment the sucking sounds began, I took off. Toward the very back of the tavern, I found a spacious booth that was looked empty. Except... I could feel there were angels here. I'd seen this before. An invisibility cloud. It stifled out sight and sound, keeping others from being able to eavesdrop or spy.

I grinned.

I found him.

I neared the edge of the cloud, putting my ear close, staying hidden so they wouldn't see me from the other side.

"The Atlanthyst Stone."

A deep, cool, confident voice slipped into the air and snaked into my chest, causing a flutter. A delicious, icy trill tickled my shoulders. I licked my lips. Was that the voice of the prince? And the Atlanthyst Stone? Why were they talking about it?

"Of all the bloody gems, he wants the Atlanthyst Stone?"

"Isn't that stone buried deep in the Pearl Palace?"

"Do you hear anything?" Kianga whispered, leaning in. "Cause we can't—"

"Shh," I hushed her, listening closer.

"How in the rot are we supposed to get into the Pearl Palace and steal the stone?"

"I have a plan."

I plucked out every hushed word spoken, growing hot with anger. How dare they try to steal the stone? Especially when I needed the burning thing if I was going to survive El'Tide!

Abruptly, the cloudy barrier disappeared. Bristling steel-grey and blue eyes looked directly at me.

"See." The angel looked at me and chuckled.

The Sea crush me with her unforgiving waves if I didn't buckle even just a little beneath the sound. This was High Prince Yakobba? Rot, he was handsome.

"Payè demands I bring Aziziens. Well, here they are."

Yakobba tilted his head, studying me.

"Wait! I was looking for you. On behalf of the princess. I am her Ayella-in-waiting. She expected to see you on her arrival, but you—"

"Don't care," he finished smoothly, splaying that cocky grin of his. It angered me to my core. His eyes flashed like quickening silver. "Engèli, take them. All three. Bring them to the *Ashweaver*."

Tobe and Kianga whipped out their tridents. A flash of light popped above our heads. A whip of mist shot out, latching onto our bodies. In a blink, Kianga, Tobe, and I were bound by chains of cloud. The big angel, Engèli, looked large enough to pulverize a platoon with his bare hands. I cursed, my panic rising.

"Release us now, you shell-eating piece of rot!"

Yakobba whistled. "So the pretty one has a temper."

"Let us go!"

"Oh, pearling, I will." His smile both aroused and enraged me at the same time. "On my ship."

High Prince Yakobba winked at me. Then Engèli reached forward, grabbed us by our chains, and dragged us away.

CHAPTER 15
DECEPTIONS AT SEA
YAKOBBA

"I can't believe you left Avari without telling the king and queen."

I looked at the ayèl floating beside me and grimaced.

"Aisha, we talked about this. This isn't my first time. They'll get over it."

Aisha frowned, her petite frame shuddering despite the heat beating down on our temples.

"It's still wrong and could cause havoc even before we get to Azizi. You shouldn't have done it, Yakobba."

"And you shouldn't be here," Nyala snapped. "Still haven't learned to stop running your mouth, I see."

Aisha's hazel and olive green eyes flashed. "Still haven't learned to stop kissing Yakobba's rhèr, I see."

Nyala snarled, shooting into the air, summoning her *ethèr*.

I groaned, tossing my head back. We'd been at sea for ten dawns and these two had remained at each other's throats the entire time.

"Cut it out and get back to work!" I barked.

Aisha hissed, whipped around, and flew to Engèli's side. He almost never left the wheel, mainly out of stubbornness, trying to prove he didn't need Aisha's help to navigate to the Azizien waterway. Nyala stared at the angel until she landed by Engèli, before spinning around and heading to the opposite end of the ship, where she tinkered with the materials to duplicate the Atlanthyst Stone.

"Bloody hells," I grumbled to myself.

"You won't succeed, you know."

I snapped my head up and found the Ayella-in-waiting floating a few paces from me. She'd begun flying, in small spurts, to practice using her wings outside of the sea.

"Good dawn to you, too, Ayella Corellis."

Corellis blushed, then glowered, annoyed at something.

"Give up this foolish quest. You'll never get your hands on the stone, High Prince."

"For the love of the skies," I growled. "Stop calling me that. You're on my ship. It's Captain Ashthorn. Use the right name or keep quiet."

I bared my teeth at her. She gasped, jumping back a step, before flattening the length of her pale blue gown. My attention snagged on the fabric as it clung to her tall, curvy frame, like liquid. Heat burrowed in my gut, but I ignore it.

"Fine, Captain Ashthorn," Corellis said. "Planning to steal the Atlanthyst Stone is suicide. You should give up the chase."

I smiled. She did not know how ballsy I was. But she'd learn.

"I'll give it up when you learn to stop walking like you have a stick shoved up your rhèr."

Jabari barked out a laugh, floating at the side of the ship, working on our cannons. His shoulders quaked as several hisses rang out.

"That is no way to speak to our Ayella!"

I looked at the tall Seaveiller and rolled my eyes. She'd been a royal pain in my rhèr since she'd snuck on to the *Ashweaver* thinking she could break the others free, only to be caught herself. I let all the sea angels roam freely, but I was wondering if that was a mistake.

I rubbed at my temples, wanting about three oversized goblets of skywine and Masaiya's curvy hips in my grasp. The insufferable heat of the sôls weren't helping. I flicked my gaze to Corellis. At least, that's what she told me her name was. I could've pressed for the truth, if there were any to be found, but that would've been a waste of my time.

"Do you need something, Ayella?"

Corellis flushed, looking to the sea. She bit her lip, as if thinking of what to say. Then she looked back, her eyes storming.

"Thank you."

I raised a brow, running a hand through my hair. I'd pushed it up into a bun when I awoke and was thankful for the decision. Corellis shifted on her feet as she looked up at me through those pretty, long lashes.

Rot.

I had to look at her without seeing her.

"Thank you," she said again, with a bit more confidence. "For allowing us to roam freely. I know Terfitti hasn't been the easiest to deal with..."

I snorted.

That was a rotting understatement. The bloody

angel had been storming around like she owned my ship. It was all I could do to keep my crew from wrapping her in spike chains and throwing her overboard in shrark infested sea.

"Thank you. Your grace doesn't go unnoticed."

I nodded at Corellis.

There was nothing else to say. Besides. Some of my crew were lingering to hear what was said, so they could be the first to spread foolish gossip. I wouldn't have it.

Corellis curtsied before floating away. She stumbled a bit, her wings unused to the weight of the sôls, but she floated all the way to the front of the ship before settling to her feet with her Seaveillers.

I leaned on the railing close to me, looking out at the sea. Engèli led us across smooth waters. The journey had been peaceful, except for the tantrums of the Seaveiller, Terfitti. Aisha worked with Engèli for us to find the fastest waterway to Azizi... when he let her. Nyala kept busy, playing with all sorts of materials that could replicate the Atlanthyst Stone. We were making good progress, crossing the Mistwind Seas with no issues. If we kept this up, we'd reach Azizi in no time.

The sounds of the crew shuffling back and forth, handling the needs of the ship, turned into a familiar hum in my ears. I watched the sea, and the life swimming beneath. Every now and again, dolfinis would swim to the surface, then burst through, singing their melodies as they flipped over themselves in the air, before diving back into the waters. The sight was breathtaking. Calming. As we continued sailing, I noticed a dark tint deep below the water's surface.

"What the rot?" I murmured.

"That's not new," Engèli called down from above. "It's been growing. Remember when we passed through the Anthuraen channel a few mekàd ago? Even then, I caught it. It goes deep."

"It looks like some kind of taint," I said, squinting to see better.

"Maybe it's a curse," Jabari called from his perch by the cannons.

Murmurs spread across the ship when they spotted the dark sludge below the waters.

The Aziziens were none too happy about it.

Corellis stared at the waters of the sea, riddled with sorrow and something akin to guilt. Her shoulders bent inward, as if she carried a heavy weight. But she had nothing to worry about. Azizi had the Atlanthyst Stone which would heal their waters and keep anything poisonous from hurting their kingdom.

My face crumpled. Rot. They wouldn't have the stone for long. Once I stole it, Azizi would have no defense. I buried the thoughts and focused outward.

I looked back to Corellis. Her eyes never left the sea. As if she could see all the way to Azizi and the Pearl Palace. A knot of guilt twisted in my gut. I buried that, too. It was her fault for eavesdropping.

My attention kept snagging on the Ayella-in-waiting. Something about her was alluring. She was quiet, usually letting her Seaveillers do most of the talking. But in her eyes, I saw a world of intelligence and curiosity. I wondered if all the sea angels were like her.

We Avariens were a chatty, rowdy, exuberant bunch. The sea angels were not the same. They talked amongst each other, and even that was done with a regal quiet. Alessayi would have a hard time with them. She liked to talk and loved it even more when the angel talked back.

Rolling up my sleeves, I floated up to the cloumàk I had Jakran and Ifu set up for me between the masts. It was the perfect spot to catch the soft breeze of the wind, while swaying as if sleeping on clouds, and getting the best view of the Mistwind Seas. I flew to the hammock, laid inside, and crossed my legs, folding my arms over my chest. I stared at the sea until it lulled me to sleep.

My eyes snapped open when a heavy thud sounded below.

"What in the rot?"

I blinked, realizing the sôlsunes had descended, and it was full-blown dusk now. I rolled over in the cloumàk, looking down, but only seeing shadows.

"Engèli," I called. "What's the word?"

"Serène," Engèli barked, his voice strained.

I laughed. That had to be a joke. The Serène hadn't bothered to show themselves in several millethium. They were practically myths. Besides, it wasn't like we'd sailed into the Serène Bergs. There was no way Engèli could be serious.

Another heavy thud rocked the ship.

A cold flutter skipped in my chest.

I hadn't been to a Temple in a hellishly long time, but I threw a fleeting prayer up to the Alpha, anyway. If there ever was a time to ask him for help, I figured now was it. We couldn't be dealing with Serène for real. We just couldn't.

I rolled out of the cloumàk, letting myself tumble until I landed perfectly on the main deck. I looked around the ship and cursed colorfully.

"No rotting way," I breathed.

Standing tall were nine Serène. They were more beautiful than I'd expected, in a broken sort of way. My jaw hung at the sight of their slender bodies. Some had light eyes, and others were dark. They all had long hair down to their calves. They were stunning... if a well-made coffin could be called that. The Serène flexed hands, ending in long claws as they rooted themselves onto the ship. Then I noticed more crawling up the sides of the *Ashweaver* as the sweetest, alluring melody filled the air, the song tugging at my hearts.

Rot, rot, rot.

"Cover your ears!" I screamed. I flexed my wings and slammed a pair over my ears to snuff all sounds from entering. If I let myself hear the song, even for a moment, I'd be dead.

I looked up at a horrifying sight, straight out of a nightmare. The Serène leading the troop tilted her head, pure hatred contorting her features. She lifted a webbed hand, pointing straight at Ayella Corellis. All the Serène turned to the sea angel and snarled viciously.

"There she is."

The Serène lifted a clawed finger in the air, then she charged.

CHAPTER 16

COLLISIONS WITH SERÈNE

RAESHELLE

I looked around the *Ashweaver* as chaos ensued. I gaped, flabbergasted at the nine Serène standing proudly to the end of the deck. Even worse, their murderous eyes were pinned on me. Rot. I hated I recognized some of those faces.

Serène were once angels of the sea before they were Clipped—having their wings broken at the taloned joints, and pierced through the bone, then plucked so they could never fly again—transfigured, then exiled for one form of treason or another. They were stripped of their true beauty, their wings, their ethereal angelic demeanor and abilities, and were cursed to be bound to the depths of the sea.

These nine had been sentenced by King Bakari.

Three of them used to be family.

"Cruesaiyi?" I whispered.

It felt as if everything on the ship had gone quiet. Like there was no one on the deck but the two of us. I looked in horror at Cruesaiyi Thesalla Reefsea, former Avarien princess, and once my favorite cousin.

"Blessed Alpha. What has become of you?"

I covered my mouth, shaking with emotion to the point of tears. I scanned the rest of the tall, gangly bodies, as strong as they were starved, with dark skin and patchy scales looking aged and worn. My hearts went out to them. I couldn't look at them without feeling immense compassion.

Cruesaiyi glared, pure hatred staining her snarling face. She lifted a clawed finger, pointed to me, and snarled.

"Se li se okea." Her sing-song voice slithered into the crisp, cold air. *"Touye yo heidät kaikki. Li se on minun."*

I froze as Cruesaiyi's words slid over my slack limbs.

She is the one. Kill them all. She is mine.

Then the Serène charged.

Kianga and Tobe were in front of me before I could blink. Around me, the sky angels launched into action, summoning their *ethèr*. With one cry from Yakobba, they charged at the Serène.

Everything was happening too fast. One moment, Yakobba wasn't far from me, his eyes glittering with rage as he assessed the Serène both on the ship, and the rest still crawling onto it. The next, the pirate prince was dancing with the Serène, cutting them down with his cutlass wrapped in *ethèr*.

I needed to do something. I needed to move. Instead, I just stood there, hyperventilating, rooted to the spot. I breathed heavily, terrified at the battle taking place around me. Searot. I was a princess, not a Sea Watcher. I didn't know what to do.

In the mayhem, Cruesaiyi locked eyes on me, cutting down the sky angels ruthlessly to get to me.

"Princess," Kianga hissed. Thank the seas the sky angels couldn't hear her. I glanced her way. "You need to get out of here, now! Go below deck and—"

A Serène shot out from the railing, having crawled onto the ship undetected, and launched herself at Kianga's back. I screamed, but it was too late. Kianga wouldn't be able to dodge the blow.

Something in me snapped. I moved, my mind going blank as my feet found purpose. In a blink, I entered my spirit plane and dropped into my wells of *ethèr*. The chasm was deep, thrumming with the cataclysmic power of the Atlanthyst Stone.

It demanded, begged, to be used. It wasn't often I used the power of the Atlanthyst Stone. I was warned against it and had heeded the warning for most of my life. It was intoxicating. All-consuming.

I drew on a contained measure of *ethèr*, channeling it into my palms, and thrust the blast at the chest of the Serène headed for Kianga. I'd caught the foul creature right before her claws had ripped my Seaveiller into shreds. The power burned the Serène like acid, disintegrating her skin before turning her into ashen stone. The Serène fell like a rock, eyes unblinking.

I didn't give her another thought. Spinning around myself, I launched into the malay.

I turned to another Serène and blasted her with the power. Forming a spear with the ethereal substance, I spun to another and cut them down mercilessly. On and on I went, spinning and cutting. I fell into an amateur dance of death like the sky angels and my Seaveillers.

Another Serène snarled, hurling themselves towards me. I lifted the spear of *ethèr*, ready to cut through them, too. Then icy claws sunk into my shoulder, breaking through skin and bone. I screeched. Tobe whipped around, cursing colorfully. He was surrounded and couldn't get to me. Kianga also let out a slew of curses. She couldn't get to me, either.

At that moment, I noticed the growing stillness on the ship. The deck was littered with many unmoving bodies. Several of those bodies belonged to Seaveillers. I felt myself going numb. The pain in my shoulder was spreading. Agony paralyzed my limbs. I doubled over, struggling to stand upright, unable to take a breath. A bitter laugh curled around my shoulders.

"Votre payè était yon moun fou, annoit sinun kite wayòm nan. Maintenant, vous aurez saat maistaa, mitä hän teki sa li te fè nou."

Your payè was a fool for letting you leave the kingdom. Now you'll get a taste of what he did to us.

"Cruesaiyi, stop this!"

"Funny. That's what I cried to King Bakari before he had me Clipped."

Cruesaiyi leapt towards me, but I was faster. I shot into the sky, wings flapping. I was unsteady in my flight, but I was also unreachable.

A howl filled the air. It was deafening, rattling the entire ship. I looked down and shrieked. The pirate prince was surrounded.

The *Ashweaver* crew fought hard, cutting down as many Serène as they could to reach the prince, but there were too many of them. Engèli, was getting tired. The swipe of his cutlass was slowing. Blood dripped down his arms and onto his breeches.

I knew a good deal of it was his.

Looking from Engèli, I found Nyala and Jabari. The two were much like Engèli. Fighting, but getting tired. And in their fatigue, the swarming Serène were landing more blows.

Yakobba howled again. The Serène battered him, tirelessly.

I couldn't bear it.

I searched for him among all of those gangly bodies, their claws swiping, their incisors biting into angelic flesh. Yakobba was in the middle on his knees. *Ethèr* swirled around him. He looked every inch the prepossessing High Prince, even as he panted, his tunic and breeches slick with blood. I looked at his face and almost laughed. Even in this moment, that stubborn edge never left his jawline. He would not give up. He would actually face death herself before cowering and giving in.

Yakobba fused his *ethèr* into his cutlass and launched into swiping off heads from shoulders. He used the small talon of his wings to cut into throats before pouring his *ethèr* into Serène bodies. The watery monstrosities began dropping to the deck like stone. The High Prince of Avari was wounded, but still fighting. Still giving everything he had. For himself, for his crew. But he was staggering. Every step he took was slower than the last.

I had to use the power of the stone. If I didn't, he wouldn't survive.

"Alpha, forgive me, but I must," I whispered, sending a prayer to the heavens, pleading for mercy for what I was about to do.

Even though the Serène were monstrosities, I found deciding to end their fallen lives, hard. The thought of killing them weighed me down.

"I'm sorry," I said, tears filling my eyes. "I'm so sorry."

I closed my eyes, pushed everything out of my mind, and drew on the power of the Atlanthyst stone. Cataclysmic power flooded my body. My eyes widened, my back arched, and my head fell backwards. The power of the Atlanthyst stone built up inside of me like an endless crescendo. Then it poured out of my hands and mouth. Sparkling light shot out of my chest, directed at every Serène, those on the deck and the ones still in the water, readying themselves to climb up the sides of the ship.

Horrifying screams filled the air.

Then Serène bodies started toppling over, lifeless.

Abruptly, the flow of power cut off, and I began tumbling to the deck of the ship.

Vaguely, I watched as Tobe pivoted to perch himself beneath me, ready to brace my fall. Then Yakobba was there, shoving him out of the way, as he flew into the air to catch me in his muscular arms. They were sticky with blood but held a warmth that caused my body to settle with ease.

"We can't continue to Azizi yet," I heard him say.

"You don't mean to bring us to—"

"That's exactly what I mean," Yakobba barked.

I didn't know who he was talking to. I didn't care. Rot, I was exhausted. Everything began fading. Darkness enveloped me. Yakobba held me with gentleness, as if he was holding feathers. He brought me close to his ribbed chest. A chill curled my toes as his last words trickled into my ears, his warm breath tickling the tips.

"We need to clean up this mess. Then we can head for Ashbone Island."

The pirate squeezed me one more time, leaning my head against his chest. I took a final breath, then tumbled into a bottomless black.

CHAPTER 17

BARGAIN WITH THE DARK

YAKOBBA

"We made it, Cap."

I looked to where Engèli pointed and grunted in satisfaction. We finally made it to Ashbone Island. Blinking, I warred against my heavy eyelids. I hadn't shut them since we left the Serène Bergs four dawns ago. I wasn't sure how much longer I could push my waning strength. Skies. I needed sleep.

Pulling up to the shoreline was a relief. Grumbling spilled over the main deck as the crew floated around, collecting what they needed for us to drop anchor. Mindless chatter, with a load of bullrot gossip, rose to my hearing.

"Bloody ashes, we've reached the accursed island."

"You think the stories are true? You think he is really here?"

"I think the moment we step foot on that island, we're not leaving."

"Oh shut up, you lout. Captain Ashthorn has been here before, more than once, and he survived."

"Yeah, but his sanity didn't."

Engèli snorted. Loud.

He'd heard them, too.

"Rotting, superstitious, karraba eaters," I grumbled, folding my arms in annoyance. "Get these blue-backed, sea worms off my ship and working. We're here for three dawns. That's it."

Engèli nodded, eyes already scanning the crew members flying scatter-brained throughout the ship.

"I don't like this."

I whipped around and found Aisha floating by my side, pretty face contorted in a deep-set frown that made me nervous. Had she seen something? What did she know that we didn't?

I hadn't seen her since we boarded and made our journey. I couldn't even remember if I saw her during the battle with the Serène.

"Where the rot have you been?"

Aisha scowled, lifting her chin as she met my gaze, glare for glare.

"This entire trip is ballsy and stupid. I'm here because we go way back, and I was willing to do you this solid. Don't question me and my work or you can get to Azizi by yourself!"

Without another word, Aisha spun on her feels, pumped her wings twice, and flew down the ramp, across the deck, off the ship, and continued onto the island, until we couldn't see her anymore.

I wanted to break something.

"I'm telling you, she can't be trusted."

I didn't bother looking at Nyala. My patience was wearing thin. With all of them. Rot. I really needed to sleep.

"I'm going to get Ayella Corellis. She should be up by now." I jutted my chin back to the crew. "Get them moving." A look to Engèli. "Get yourself ready. Cause we're going in the Wood."

Engèli's nostrils flared as I turned around, flew to my cabin and went to wake up the Ayella from the sea.

THE SHORE WAS SILENT AS THE GRAVE AS ENGÈLI AND I

floated several paces from the entrance to the Poisoned Wood.

"You know I'm right behind you once you fly in, Cap."

I threw an unimpressed glance at Engèli. He grinned but made no move to fly into the Wood first. The thick, dark forest loomed high and menacing. It took up nearly the entire island, with trees coated in black leaves and emerald sap oozing out of their bark.

Engèli didn't budge.

Coward.

The *Ashweaver* angels floated several paces behind us, Nyala and Jabari perched at their lead. Both had refused to come. They insisted their presence was needed on shore. Nyala emphasized the importance of her making sure repairs to the damaged parts of the ship remained on schedule.

I was a pirate captain of a bunch of rotting cowards.

"Are you sure we have to go?"

My chest squeezed at the accented, melodic voice. Curious, unsure, but elegant and serene. The voice belonging to one who could sit on any throne, and command armies at will. Ayella Corellis floated to my left. It had been stupid of me to tell her what

Engèli and I were going to do. The moment she heard, she demanded to come along. When Corellis said she was coming, Kianga declared she was coming, too.

Engèli was more than happy for Kianga to join us. He looked at her now, eyebrows wriggling at her as she scrunched her nose at him. Skies. When Engèli marked an angel, he never let up. I was of half a mind to tell him to back off. But Kianga was a Seaveiller of the Pearl Palace. If she could handle King Au'Pearls court, she could handle Engèli.

"We already discussed this. We must," I answer Corellis.

My attention snagged on the flutter of her pale blue gown, lifting with the eery breeze floating from the Poisoned Wood. A thin barrier of old *ethèr* surrounded the Wood. It was said that was the only thing that kept the Konda King from breaking free. I thought it was all a bunch of rot.

"I need alluniem for the hull or else *Ashweaver* isn't making it to Azizi."

"And the stores of alluniem are in the bowels of the Poisoned Wood's caves," Engèli added.

Kianga shivered and said, "I don't like it."

"Then you can stay, Ayella," I grinned down at her.

Kianga hissed. The sound made Corellis twitch her ears. The slight movement triggered a spike of heat through my chest so hard I nearly went blind from it. I yanked my gaze away, fighting for air.

"Let's go."

I crossed the invisible barrier and flew into the Poisoned Wood.

The first sensation to hit me was the stench of old in the air.

"It's quiet," Engèli remarked.

"Too quiet," I agreed.

"I don't like it," Kianga grumbled.

There was no sound. No flutter of the leaves. Nor chirping of birds. No scuttling of furry creatures littering the floor. There wasn't a sound but the breath coming out of my mouth.

"I have the same feeling I get when I see Sea Watchers in the Pearl Palace," Corellis murmured.

I turned to her and found that she'd drawn on her *ethèr*. I studied her hands. They were sparkled with a white mist that curled around her wrists as tiny water droplets fell from them.

Something about her *ethèr* pulled at me. It drew me like bait on a hook. My chest squeezed as I fought to look away. I shook my head, forcing the urge out of me. Skies. What kind of *ethèr* was that?

Kianga had her own mist stirring, shifting between sea blues and foam greens, curling up her arms as she expertly took in every detail of the Wood. Both sea angels floated, their watery, membranous wings flapping in the quiet.

I couldn't stop looking at Corellis. I noted her erect posture, inquisitive blue and silver eyes, and her courtly grace. She was an Ayella-in-waiting, probably with several lords waiting on her hand back in Azizi. Assuming I brought her back alive. I sneered. The thought of a sea lord taking her hand to bond with her as soulu set me ablaze with an unhinged sort of anger.

"Cap," Engèli called, snapping me out of it.

I turned to find him watching me, amused. Luckily, he kept his mouth shut. He pointed through the trees. "There they are. The Peaks. The caves are there."

I nodded, glad to have my focus back on our mission.

"We can get there in a few hôrs if we fly without breaks."

"Without breaks?" Corellis blurted out.

My eyes fell on her pretty, curly ivory hair brushing past her shoulders.

"Ayella Corellis, it isn't too late for you to return

to—"

"No." She lifted her chin. "I'm coming with you."

Her eyes pierced into me. With a flick of her gaze, she found Engèli watching and grinning. Her cheeks flushed. It was hard not to lean down and do something stupid.

I jerked away, unable to talk past the stiffness in my throat. Without another word, we pressed into the thick of the trees.

Hôrs began going by. The blackened leaves fell to the forest floor like rain.

"This bloody, insufferable heat," Kianga muttered, summoning water into her palms and spraying herself, before going back to clearing trees from her path.

I had to agree. It was hot. I unbuttoned my tunic and rolled up my sleeves. I took another swig of water, then began cutting down more branches. It felt as if the Poisoned Wood was fighting our journey. The closer we pressed to the peaks, the tougher it became to navigate the dense forest.

"Really, you sky angels live in misery," Kianga grumbled.

Engèli and I glanced at her. The sea angel was wheezing. Her shoulders shook, her arms pulsing with strain. Sweat pooled down the thin, skin-clad armor she wore, as her matted hair clung to the nape of her neck. She checked on Corellis often, making sure the Ayella was alright. Kianga bent over, panting, the effort visible in her taut limbs.

I wanted to slow for them, but I couldn't. We needed to get in and out of the caves before the sôlsunes were gone. Staying inside the wood during the dusk could prove fatal. We didn't have time to rest. I flickered a concerned look to Engèli. His eyes were glued to Kianga, his lips bowed in a deep frown.

"I know this is... a challenge," I started, trying my best at empathy. I failed to keep the irritation out of my voice, though. If they had bloody listened, they would still be on the shore right now with the crew, while Engèli and I could press on to the caves. "But we're almost there." That was a blatant lie, but it would have to do. They had to keep flying. "It's too late to head back and—"

"We don't need your sympathy, pirate," Kianga snapped. "We're tired, not dying. Once we catch our breath, we'll be on our rotting way."

Engèli snorted, nostrils flaring at her attitude. A low rumble left his throat that made Kianga snap her head at him. Her eyes enlarged, but her jaw only hardened.

"Tread lightly, pretty one." His eyes glittered as his voice grew to a dangerous quiet. "You're addressing my captain and the High Prince of Avari. I will kill you where you fly if I must."

I grew still in the tension.

Kianga's eyes burned with rage. Engèli grew unnaturally still, eyes glued to the sea angel.

"Guys, what was that?" Corellis squeaked. "I think... I think," she stuttered, eyes only widening the longer she stared at the distance. Then she began squealing. "FLY!"

Corellis snapped her wings and raced off into the trees. What in the rot? I was about to think her mad when I heard it.

Heavy stomps pounding into marshy ground.

I shared a glance with Engèli.

"The Konda King," we said at the same time.

Then a roaring hiss crackled through the air, chilling my spine down to my toes. Without another word, I snapped my wings and shot into the trees like lightning, Engèli in tow. Kianga had already taken off the moment the cry filled the air.

"Etheriens," a crawling, cold voice hissed.

I felt more than heard the words. The depth of hatred every syllable carried made my hearts pound faster. The deafening stomps were growing closer, and it seemed we were nowhere nearer to the bloody caves.

"We won't make it," I whispered to myself. Realization hit me. If we kept at this speed, the Konda would reach us and kill us. I yelled out to Engèli.

"Grab Kianga, now!"

I shot forward, wrapped my arms around Corellis, slammed her close to my chest, and shot through the trees at full speed. Engèli grabbed Kianga and kept close to my heels. We flew like our lives depended on it. Before I knew it, with the lingering hiss of the Konda King in tow, we reached the peaks and plunged into the mouth of the caves.

CHAPTER 18
FACING THE KONDA KING
YAKOBBA

"Yakobba!" Corellis squealed as I raced through the darkness of the caves.

"I've got you, Corellis. Hang tight."

Engèli and I flew hard, racing across the caves. We followed the columns until we reached an underwater pool. The bed of the pool was littered with precious gems.

I didn't blink twice at the opulence. I was focused on one thing.

Getting alluniem.

My six hearts strained with the force of the flight, but I couldn't stop. The caves were quiet. Peaceful. One could almost forget it was the home of the Konda King.

Almost.

Corellis gripped my arms. I felt her hearts racing. She trembled against my chest. I heard her heavy breathing and smelled the sweat dripping down her skin.

I fought my arousal at having her pressed so close to me. I shook my head and flew harder. Distractions now would only get us both killed.

"Corellis, I need a favor."

"What do you need, pirate prince?"

"I prefer Captain Ashthorn."

"Yeah? And I prefer not to be hunted by monsters that shouldn't exist."

My nostrils flared, my eyebrows climbing. I squeezed her waist. I smiled in triumph at her small squeal.

"Prissy little thing. You've picked a good time to find your tongue."

Corellis stiffened in my arms.

Bam.

I howled, our flight dipping, nearly sending us plunging into the waters below, as pain shot up my knee from where she'd kicked me. For an Ayella so small, she could kick really hard.

"Bloody hells," I wheezed, my leg throbbing. I

snapped my wings to force our flight straight again, curving through the massive cave.

"You okay, Cap?" Engèli asked.

"I've got a pretty damsel in my arms, needing me to save her, my good friend. I've never been better."

Engèli howled with laughter. Corellis hissed. Her body shifted. I had just a moment to move my legs, before she slammed both her feet into empty air and cursed, slamming my arms with her webbed hands.

"And she also has a temper!"

"Keep it going and I'll aim for what keeps you an ayèn next."

I gasped and shut my mouth. I had a feeling she'd do it for real.

Suddenly, Engèli was speaking with a tight voice.

"I don't know how much I enjoy being a hero for a thankless damsel, Cap."

I snorted. Kianga and Corellis were practically the same. For Engèli's sake, I hoped Kianga had only gone for his knees, too.

Ungrateful ayèl.

Our flight brought us into the first of many caves that were buried in the bowels of the Poisoned Peaks. When we crossed into its center, I sighed, looking around in awe. I'd been here only twice.

Each time, my breath was taken away. Corellis gasped.

"What in all the seas of Mistwind?" she breathed.

Reflexively, I squeezed her waist, brushing her dress above her stomach with my thumb. She shivered at the touch, pressing into me. I held her tight as I came to a float. I could've let her go now that we were here. Could've released her to fly on her own and look around. I didn't. I saw Engèli didn't release Kianga either. What was more surprising, the Seaveiller wasn't putting up a fight for him to release her, either.

Every inch of the cave was covered in celestial metal. Alluniem was an ancient metal from another cosm, but its origins were unknown. It was one of the strongest metal I'd gotten my hands. I often wondered about the planet it must have come from. Avariens were forced to come here en masse, many often dying, to collect the metal for Avarien labor throughout the kingdom.

I unwound my wings, using a free hand to reach for a large satchel I'd folded and tucked into my onyx cloak. Engèli pulled out the same. We flew to the walls and reached out a hand when—

"I want to do it," Corellis said. Her melodic voice

filled the cavern. Kianga echoed the sentiment. Engèli and I shared a look before I shrugged.

"Swear to no more kicks."

Corellis whipped her head around as far as she could, glaring.

"You're not serious."

"Swear you won't be aiming for my gonzos or you don't get to touch the alluniem."

Her nose scrunched in the cutest fashion. Self control was a feat. Skies. I wanted to kiss her. Bad.

Corellis batted pretty lashes up at me, her face painted with mock innocence.

"I swear it on the name of King Au'Pearl, may he reign until the Ellelights take him, that I will not kick anymore... on purpose."

Corellis flashed a smile that made my chest squeeze. I nodded, gave her the bag, and flew close to the walls. Using my cutlass in my free hand, I chipped away at big chunks of the alluniem, waiting for her to collect them, before chipping away at more.

The cave filled with the sounds of Engèli and me chipping until the satchels were full. Engèli and I both used a pair of our wings to sweep below the sea angels so we could help them carry the satchels.

"Time to go," I said, flying back from the wall.

Engèli grunted in agreement.

"Go where exactly?"

Both ayèls squealed as Engèli and I whipped around. The Konda King perched low to the ground with his massive, serpentine body balanced on four legs, ending in clawed, reptilian feet.

"What in the seas!" Kianga cried.

"Oh my seas," Corellis chorused, flaring my hate for the Konda King. I hated hearing that small, terrified voice from her. "Oh my seas," she cried.

I didn't have to look to know the Ayella-In-Waiting was crying. Primal, protective rage flared through my blood. I snarled at the Konda King, flooding the *ethèr* into my palms. Engèli and I leaned forward, ready to barrel through this beast to get out. We would have to maneuver past the konda.

I looked at his scales. They gleamed in the light of the beaming metal surrounding us. It was said they were forged in the fires of the Black Hells themselves. Nothing could penetrate those scales.

I shared another look with Engèli. He nodded. We had to be smart about this. Going on offense would get us all killed. To make it out alive, we had to go on defense and find a way past the beast.

As if sensing our plan, the Konda King sat on his haunches, spreading the length of his body across the opening. He blinked at me, golden serpentine eyes gleaming.

"High Prince Yakobba," He hissed. "Heir to the Avarien throne, Brightstar of the skies, parading around as a false pirate in the hopes your greedy king will remember he spawned more than one prince."

I flinched as if I'd been punched in the face. Emotions stormed me, threatening to undo me. My ears burned. I ground my teeth, eyes still desperately searching for a way out.

"Silence, you devilish spawn of the Black Hells," Kianga hissed. "We've heard of you in the sea. You are the one masquerading about, pretending to be other from what you are. I am not so easily swayed by legend. My payè told me the truth." We all had our eyes glued to Kianga as she boldly glared at the Konda King. "You are no Konda King," Kianga sneered.

"But of course he is," Corellis whispered, as if she and Kianga were in a private discussion. "It's plain and obvious, Kia!"

"No, he's not, Ayella," Kianga said, still glaring at the enormous serpent whose eyes had gone from burnished gold to darkened midnight. "The Konda King is actually a Fallen!"

The Konda King lunged.

Engèli and I snapped our wings and dove. As if in slow motion, Engèli and I flew beneath the scaly body of the konda, hardly avoiding the long claws of his hands and feet. As the konda roared, Engèli and I shot for the opening, narrowly avoiding the Konda's poisoned tail.

"Fly, Gèli. FLY!"

Engèli and I flew with unnatural speed, our arms wrapped tight around the sea angels holding the satchels full of alluniem. We flew back through the caves. The walls rattled with the screeching hiss of the Konda King. We kept flying until we plunged back into the blighted forest.

Sôlight still hung overhead. Losing myself in the flight, I leaned into adrenaline and hyper speed. I flew through the Poisoned Wood, racing back to shore. I saw nothing. Heard nothing. I tumbled into a void and flew.

I didn't remember when I plunged through the barrier surrounding the Wood. But even then, I didn't stop flying. Corellis was screaming. At some point, she released her grip on the satchel, letting it fall into the hands of my pirates. She yelled for me to stop flying, but I couldn't hear her. I was lost in the void and couldn't snap out of it.

Skies.

I was so tired.

Our flight didn't end until I'd flown to the Mistwind Sea and tumbled into the water. I released Corellis and felt myself sinking. I sensed her swimming towards me. By the time I felt the gentle strokes of webbed hands, I'd tumbled into endless black and was swept into the deep.

CHAPTER 19
WOO THE BEAUTY OF THE SEA
RAESHELLE

"How is he?"

I looked up and met Engèli's striking, pale and hazel eyes. He squatted next to me, drooping his wings into the sand. I threw a look back at the erected tent behind us where the pirate prince slept. Two dawns had gone, and he hadn't awakened. I turned back to Engèli.

"Better. He tosses when he sleeps," I smiled to myself. "I think he has nightmares, but when he moves, it comforts me. I know he's alive. I hope he awakes this dawn."

Engèli nodded. He looked out at the sea. For a moment, we sat there in silence.

"Thank you."

"For?"

"Keeping an eye on him."

I flushed. Trailing the rolling tides, I nodded in response.

"You don't have to, you know? We can easily take over and—"

"I want to," I cut in. "He's like this because he was protecting me. If it wasn't for him... wasn't for you, Kianga and I..." I trailed off, unable to finish.

I lifted my eyes to Engèli, his colossal frame blocking out the sôlight. Since we'd made it out of the Poisoned Wood, I noticed he kept doing that for Kianga and I. He must have said something, because the remaining crew would conveniently find themselves close to my Seaveillers, blocking the sôlight from them as well.

Terfitti was the only one who complained.

"I owe the High Prince—"

I sucked in a sharp breath. I had to stop saying that. Yakobba hated it. After what he'd just done, I had to stop saying it.

"Captain Ashthorn saved my life. I won't allow anyone to be the first to see him." I looked at him again. "Not even you."

Engèli grinned, the smile reaching his ears.

"Aye, Ayella. If you say so." Engèli's eyes twinkled with knowing. "Well, if he wakes up or not, we need to sail this dawn. Kianga will grab your things, then if I have to drag the captain out myself, I will."

"You won't be dragging anything."

Engèli and I whipped.

High Prince Yakobba floated behind us looking more rested than he'd been in dawns. The camp fell silent. Everyone watched him. The pirate prince only had eyes for one angel. Flushing, I ignored the stares, and Engèli's low chuckling, to float up to the prince.

"Captain Ashthorn."

Yakobba's light eyes bored into mine. He didn't blink. Didn't breathe. Just stared, trailing my float until I stopped in front of him, looking up into his eyes. "Thank you."

I didn't know how to begin, fumbling for words like I did when I was a youngling. I felt foolish, but I was so overwhelmed. By now, everyone knew the story and all of its details, save a few Engèli purposefully left out. If it wasn't for him, I wouldn't have gotten out alive. I would have been taken by the Konda King. No. By the Fallen.

The prince saved me, and it did something to me. Something changed. Even Kianga felt it. She was still snippy with Engèli, but it was all playful. Her bark was gone. And so was mine.

How was I supposed to keep him from the Atlanthyst Stone now? How would I sway him? Did I even want to anymore? Rot. I felt myself swaying under the heat. Without thinking, the pirate prince spread his wings, lifting them to shield me from the sôlsunes. My hearts swelled.

"Thank you, Yakobba," I blinked up at him. "For safe passage. Defending me from the Serène. Saving me from the..." I couldn't say it. My shoulders quivered at the thought of scales, claws, and large, golden eyes.

A ringed finger lifted my chin. When my eyes met Yakobba's, his were dancing.

"Between you and me," he whispered. "I would do it all over again."

He winked, and my knees wobbled.

My chest squeezed. He brushed a few strands of my hair from my face, pushing them back behind my ears. Before I could stop myself, I leaned forward and planted a light kiss on his cheek. I pulled back, body chilled, humming with a dizzying feeling.

Yakobba grew impossibly still. His eyes grew molten. Delicious cold swept through my body. A cough sounded somewhere behind us.

Neither of us moved.

Yakobba watched me, unblinking. His limbs

were taut with need. It would be impossible sabotaging his quest now. I couldn't for the life of me take my eyes off of him. The Poisoned Wood had changed us. I wanted to know this pirate prince. I wanted to taste him, too.

The taut vein in his neck only proved he desired the same. My lips curled into a sweet, demure smile. His nostrils flared, his eyes dropping to my mouth.

"Thank you," he said, his voice all husky breath. "For watching me."

"Between you and me," I said, leaning forward like we were exchanging secrets. "I'd do it all over again."

I winked at him.

This time the pirate prince grinned, so wide it filled his face. My chest seized to the point of bursting. Blessed seas! He was so burning handsome.

Yakobba looked as if weights had fallen from his shoulders. Like this, he seemed very much the young, mischievous, trouble making prince.

I opened my mouth to say something else when a screech filled the sky.

We all turned around, heads tilted upward. An enormous beast with ivory, feathered wings, a long golden beak, with matching eyes and amber talons, hovered above. The flying creature never landed, and the ayèl never got off, keeping her own wings tucked into her spine.

"Aisha, what in the rot are you doing?" Yakobba snarled.

I glanced at him. The way he stood made him look ready to fight. I looked back at the ayèl above. Wasn't she part of his crew? He needed her to accomplish this heist successfully.

"And how the rot did you get your hands on a stareagle?"

Aisha lifted her chin.

"It's my job to have connections."

Her Avarien accent was thick. I had to strain to understand her. Her eyes were hardened as she looked from Engèli to Yakobba.

"High Prince."

Several of the *Ashweaver* crew snarled at her. Yakobba stiffened beside me but said nothing. Engèli seemed to glow. It took a moment for me to realize he was drawing on his *ethèr*. When it was clear Yakobba would not respond to her, she continued talking. Her voice shook, but she pressed on.

"I'm bowing out. I won't risk war with the Aziziens. Sea angels are vicious." Her eyes fell on the frowning Seaveillers. "No offense." She looked back to Yakobba as it was my turn to bristle at her rude statement. Vicious? We were a dominant kingdom for a reason.

But vicious? I shifted irritably.

"I'm ending here. I won't enter Azizi with you. You want the Atlanthyst Stone, you'll have to find it yourself. I can't risk being attached to war with the sea kingdom."

Yakobba said nothing for a long time. I subtly floated closer to him and brushed his hand with mind. Something like an electric shock leapt through our hands, fading just as quickly. He didn't face me, but I could feel Yakobba's pull to me. Feel him drawing from me.

The moment I pulled away, he floated up into the sky. We all watched Yakobba and Aisha. The storm in his steel eyes told me he had so much to say. He titled his head to the side, studying Aisha.

"So be it. You have not failed your captain this dawn." Yakobba rose his voice. His eyes shook violently like thunder storms. "You have failed your king."

The *Ashweaver* crew glared at her. Aisha lifted her chin as tears streamed down her cheeks. Without another word, Aisha dug her heels into the sides of the stareagle, then she was flying off, headed west.

Yakobba floated back down, the ease he had on his face moments ago, gone. The hardened pirate had returned. Wretched ayèl. I silently cursed Aisha for bringing back his foul mood.

Yakobba started barking orders.

"I heard enough to know we're ready to go. So move! Aisha leaving changes nothing." He paused, looking across the sandy shore at them all. "Unless any of you are also ready to bow out."

"Never!"

"We'll not be made into cowards."

"We sail for Azizi!"

Yakobba nodded pleasantly at their cheers. He jerked his chin to the *Ashweaver*. "Aboard you go!"

A chorus of "aye" rang through the air as the crew quickly grabbed whatever was left on the beach and flew to the ship to finish loading. Yakobba floated over to me, those piercing eyes locked on me again. I shivered under their weight.

"Here." He took my hand with a gentleness that softened all of my hearts. "This was my mamè's until she passed it to me. It's one of my payè's signet rings. Wear it. Keep it. Once we're back on the sea, the crew will see it and leave you be. Go wherever you'd like. Leave the ship and swim." His eyes glowed.

I could've folded over crying there and then. He wasn't done.

"You're a guest, not a prisoner on my ship. I am no fan of captives. You're free, Ayella. I want you to know that. You're not shackled to the deck, or your cabin. You're free. This is just a token to keep you from prying questions. Anything you answer should be on a need-to-know basis."

He winked at me, brushed his lips over my knuckles, and spun away to help his crew gather the remaining items. I was rooted to the spot with his signet ring weighing down my index finger.

I was apt to stay there and just watch him until I heard Engèli's laughter. When I turned to him, everything about him was dancing like he was in on a secret about me I'd never know. Then his grin stretched. I flew off to find Kianga with Engèli's booming laugh trailing me all the way.

CHAPTER 20
A GRAVEYARD OF LIES AND TREACHERY
RAESHELLE

Leaping off the ledge of the *Ashweaver*, I dove into the waters of the Mistwind Sea. Kianga and Terfitti jumped in after me. My sea-sight kicked in. Life below the surface unveiled itself. I breathed in the water, letting it flood my lungs and remind me of home.

"Race you." I grinned at them both.

"As if you could actually beat me," Kianga taunted. Without another word, she was shooting down through the water, rushing for the turtu reefs below.

"Cheater!" I called, racing after her.

I laughed as I swam past Kianga, neared Terfitti until I overtook her, and swam past her completely. I held my hands in front of me, as if I was flying through the water, pushing hard for the reefs. Yakobba's signet ring beamed marvelously in the water. I couldn't suppress my giddiness. It was stunning and had been his mamè's. Now it was on my finger. I blushed at the message it sent. At what that message meant.

As I swam for the turtu reefs, I realized this was the first time I actually felt free. Free to swim. To experience. To live.

I spun around myself, enjoying the sea like I'd spent a lifetime wanting to do. I reached the turtu reefs first, shrieking my victory. Seven long heartbeats passed before Kianga reached me. A few more after that and Terfitti finally arrived. I was too full in my spirit to gloat. The moment Terfitti reached us, I spun around.

"Come on! Let's see if we can find a turtu."

"We should probably leave them alone, princess," Terfitti said, warily.

I ignored her. Terfitti had always been nervous around the turtu. I never learned the reason, and I didn't care. I loved turtu and I planned to find one this dawn.

Schools of fish were here, as well as several dolfini pods. I swam below oversized mushrooms that looked almost like angelic estates, their roots embedded into sea boulders. Kianga pulled up to my right, Terfitti to the left, as we swam through the beauty of the sea. My wings propelled me forward as I quietly took it all in.

"Our home is beautiful," Kianga whispered.

Terfitti and I nodded, lost in the sea's glory. So many fish passed us by in colors of reds and oranges, yellows and blues, greens and purples. I yelped as a massive karraba swam out of his hiding spot, rushing away. Moments later, a bigger fish crashed into where he had just been, chomping on nothing but sea and weeds. I laughed, trailing the karraba still in flight, scurrying to another hiding spot.

As we swam, the sea seemed to step aside, making way for us. I kept going until we reached the dolfini pods. They looked at me with ancient wisdom in their dark eyes, their ivory blubber shining under iridescent jewels that lined their spines. They looked similar to the dolfini that swam close to the castle back home.

I lifted a hand, waving, then I sang a lullaby, slow and melodic. The dolfini spun around themselves and sung back. We carried on that way, singing back and forth, until I felt a tug at my elbows.

"Time to go," Kianga said.

I looked at the dolfini.

"Goodbye, my friends. It was good seeing you. I won't soon forget you."

They chirped in song, speaking in unison.

"Goodbye, Dayè of the King, Pearl of the Sea. Worry not. We will see you again."

My eyes welled with tears. If only they knew I was a few dawns away from eternal death. I forced a smile. My hearts ached as we turned from them, swimming without stopping until we were back at the Surface, slipping on our etheriscs, and scaling the ship to climb on. Back on deck, Tobe and Zukon floated over.

"Stand still," Zukon said quietly. He and Tobe spread their wings, flapping them in rapid succession, fanning Terfitti, Kianga, and myself until we were bone dry. I could only imagine what my hair looked like.

I shook myself, not bothering to put on sandals. I looked up at Yakobba. He was above deck, leaning on the railing. His eyes glowed, as if he'd been watching me the entire time.

I walked to him, even taking the stairs. I made it a priority to keep exercising my walking abilities. While Terfitti, Tobe, and Zukon still struggled to stay on their feet, Kianga and I were comfortable on ours.

"Enjoyed your swim?"

Yakobba smiled in a way that made my hearts dance. One could almost forget he wasn't headed straight for the Pearl Palace to steal the Atlanthyst Stone. I almost laughed. As if he'd ever get his hands on it.

"I always do." I looked at the sea. "Thank you for letting me and my Seaveillers swim freely. It means the world to us. I know the princess will appreciate it and thank you immensely for treating us so well."

"Will she?" He said, eyes glittering. "I will accept all thanks in the form of my weight in Azizien gold."

I snorted, busting out laughing.

"I remember King Rhòdhaire saying you didn't have a choice in bringing us with you. If anything, you should offer thanks in gold to spare your head from the king's trident."

Yakobba grinned wickedly, slipping closer.

"I'll admit I've never been one to fear the command of a king."

I leaned close, whispering with a sultry breath.

"Yet here you sail, rushing like a fool to do the impossible for yours."

His eyes shifted, something vulnerable filling them. For a moment, it was as if we were the only two on the entire ship.

"I have to Corellis." He blinked, his eyes swelling with an innocence I hadn't witnessed until now. This was the true Yakobba. Not the pirate, nor even the prince. This was him. I closed the gap between us, whispering back.

"Why? Are there no other ways to please the king?"

Yakobba flinched, blinking at me.

"I know you're not after the stone for yourself, Yakobba." I tilted my head. "Why this? Why the stone? When you know Azizi needs it to survive? Surely there has to be another way."

"There is none, Corellis. My mamè birthed the king two soès." He looked somewhere behind me, his voice lowering. "Perhaps once I've brought him the stone, he'll remember more than one still breathes and desires to be known by him. And maybe one dawn, even be loved by him, too."

He finished with his voice so small, so broken, I could feel my own hearts splintering. I placed my hands on his chest, looking up into his eyes. Those storms of steel fell on me, filled with a wound so deep, so raw, it tore open my chest and left me bleeding for him.

"This heist can get you killed, Yakobba," I whisper. "Surely dying isn't worth it."

"If it means he will stop cursing the dawn mamè held me in her arms and showed me to him, then yes, even death is worth it."

Witnessing such a brokenness undid something in me. I wrestled with my shame, frowning at myself. His ringed finger gently lifted my chin.

"What ails you, Ayella of the sea?"

I leaned into him, miserable. I couldn't just tell him the truth. Kianga had warned me to keep my mouth shut. She didn't care what I was, or wasn't, feeling for him. I was not about to tell him the truth. Ever. He'd find out eventually, but by then it would be too late.

I longed for these moments. He never cared if his crew stared while he acted as if we were alone. It made me feel what I'd never felt in all my life. I hated every moment that brought me closer to when this would all end.

"I know how you can get to the palace without having to go through the ports." I swallowed. "King Au'Pearl, and several sea lords, enter and leave by sumaren directly from the Pearl Palace through a waterway only royals use. I have a feeling this is how your family will be brought to the Pearl Palace. I can direct you that way to save time."

"I don't like this melancholy note your voice has

taken." Yakobba squeezed my waist, lifting my chin. He was so close I could push up on my toes and kiss him. He seemed to think the same. His eyes darkened, making my toes curl with ice. He took a long, shaky breath before speaking again.

"Maybe not now, but eventually, will you tell me what's wrong?" He touched the spot on my dress right where my hearts would be. "Here." He lifted a hand to touch my temple. "Not here." His lips spread into a crooked smile that made my hearts flutter. "We can't both be broken, Ayella. I'd rather it be me. In every cycle, in every cosm, in every realm, never you. Always me."

"I will," I said around the lump in my throat. "Well, I think I should find Engèli and show him the waterway, yes?"

I slipped out of Yakobba's grip, hating the empty feeling that came with being away from him. I rushed down the steps, searching determinedly for Engèli before I did something stupid. As I found Engèli, I was keenly aware of a pair of steel-blue and silver eyes trailing my every step.

CHAPTER 21
ENTERING THE HOME OF THE SEA
YAKOBBA

"The portal entry's up ahead."

Engèli nodded, looking at the churning whirlpool in the distance. Corellis stood beside him, shifting from foot to foot. I couldn't help but drink in her beauty. Soon enough, we'd be going our separate ways. I frowned. We ran out of time. With the setback on Ashbone Island, we'd be arriving at Azizi at the same time as the Avariens.

Brushing a hand over my beard, I floated above the quarterdeck overlooking the crew. They were in high spirits expecting the reality of the heist now that we were going to cross into Azizi territory. I could see nervousness pulling their shoulders taut and making their expressions anxious. But they were ready.

"Alright mates, listen up!" I called.

Every head lifted, all attention on me.

"We've had a harrowing journey, racing against time to get to Azizi while the Avariens made their way down for El'Tide."

Several nods trickled throughout the crew as the rest twitched the winged curves of their ears, their wings fluttering gently beneath the bright dawn.

"We've had our losses during this time," I continued, frowning as I thought of our dead, seeing their names and faces plain as a new dawn in my mind. I noticed the sea angels bowing their own heads, faces tightened in grief.

Another tally to give me.

I looked out sternly.

"You've had your chance to fly off, and I wouldn't have held it against you."

"Yes, you would have, Cap!" Jakran called.

The corner of my lips twitched.

"No, I wouldn't." A beat. "But I would have your wings plucked on sight If I ever crossed you again."

That got them laughing. The sea angels looked nervous, brows rising high. They didn't seem to think that was too funny. Corellis didn't laugh either, but her eyes were shining, and that was enough for me.

"Thank you," I said fondly. "For staying with me. We all know I carry the least desirable reputation across the sea and sky. But you've remained. And now, we have a stone to fetch."

"Like a pretty Ayella in silks?" asked Ifu.

I grinned back, winking at him. "Like a pretty Ayella in silk."

"Well, that'll motivate any ayèn, I think," called Dakri. "It sure as rot is motivating me."

Cackles broke out across the deck. Even Nyala cracked a rueful grin, shaking her head.

"All of you will remain on the *Ashweaver*, except for Hezron." I nodded at the cabin ayèn. He and I had already spoken of what I needed him to do once we were in the palace. Hezron floated on the deck below, scrubbing towel in hand, grinning like a fool.

"Ayella Corellis has been kind enough to help Engèli navigate through a waterway that will take us directly to the palace. There, we'll hide the ship in the caves below. I need all of you to be ready. We'll sail fast. If things go my way, we'll be in and out of the palace before King Au'Pearl has had enough wine to warm his entrails. The moment we board again, we take off through the same waterway and scat. All clear?"

"Aye!" the angels chorused. "All clear, Captain Ashthorn!"

"Good," I said. "Etheriscs on! We travel below sea!"

Engèli navigated the *Ashweaver* over the calm surface of the Mistwind Sea. The blues and lavenders were breathtaking. Even hints of orange danced like sparkling flecks wherever the sôlight touched.

Engèli turned the wheel, thrust it upward, then bent it back, making it almost flat. I had just enough time to slip on my etherisc when the *Ashweaver* pitched forward and plunged into the sea.

The first thing to hit me was the freezing cold. My body spasmed, wanting to fly out and get above water. A small hand came to my shoulder, reaching for the nape of my cloak. When I turned, I found Ayella Corellis trying to take my cloak off. She was resplendent, enveloped in the blues and lavenders of the sea. Her pale blue dress seemed to mold with the surrounding water, as her ivory curls floated around her shoulders.

"You'll swim better without this massive thing on you. It will slow you down."

I only nodded, listening, but moving slowly, so

she was forced to take more time helping me. I loved her touch, her scent, and wanted to keep her as close as possible. When she inevitably pulled away, my hearts rebelled.

Engèli wasted no time. He pushed a lever, thrusting the ship into high gear. Before long, we were zooming past miles of deep sea. Floating through the water, while somehow staying on the deck, I pulled away from the Ayella to bark orders at the crew.

"Draw in the masts! Quickly! Move!"

The crew rushed to obey. The sky angels struggled with dancing between floating and swimming to get their jobs done. It made for an amusing sight, but I had no time to dwell on it. A gong beat in my chest. I fisted my hands and released them before half floating, half swimming to reach Engèli.

"How much longer?"

Engèli grunted. "A few hôrs."

"How behind my payè are we?"

Engèli's lips pressed into a thin line. "Probably an entire dawn."

I threw my head back, fighting with everything I had to not explode.

"Okay, so we have to make a couple pivots," Nyala

said, floating to perch below my elbow. "That doesn't mean we won't get our hands on that stone."

She was right. There was still time and opportunity to achieve the impossible. I thought of King Izakaya getting to Azizi, not seeing me, and pitching a dangerous fit. Skies. We had to get there fast.

I looked outside of the ship. The waters were clear and beautiful. If we had the time, I'd ask Corellis to take me for a swim. I scanned the ship and found her talking furiously with her Seaveillers.

Something about it gnawed at me.

Once we arrived, she'd be out of my life as quickly as she entered it. I didn't like that at all, but I also had no way of changing it. I watched her for so long I could see when her expression darkened. When she looked out at the sea and hated what she saw. I turned with her and found the waters almost like blackened pools.

"What in the rot?" I muttered.

"I don't like this, Cap." Engèli's *ethèr* surfaced reflexively, swirling around him protectively. "Something about this is off."

The waters grew rough. I planted myself where I was as the *Ashweaver* burst out of the waterway. In the distance, a magnificent palace made of pearl, gems, and glass, surrounded by corals and perched on a high mound of ancient boulders, stood proud.

"There it is," I whispered.

Jabari whistled. "That's a palace, alright."

"We're getting close!" I shouted. "Ready yourselves."

"Aye, Captain!"

Motivated by sights of the looming palace, Engèli thrust ahead. I had eyes for nothing now except the Pearl Palace. Somewhere in there was the Atlanthyst Stone. In there was my ticket to having my payè love me like he did Ishaèli. Somewhere in there was a stone that would give me the one thing in all the blasted Elledelle realms that I wanted most. Wetting my lips, I hungered for the stone. I could practically feel it in my hands. I could almost see myself handing it over to King Rhòdhaire.

"Soon, we will say goodbye, pirate prince."

I whipped around and found Corellis beside me. Nyala was gone. Engèli made it his business to study the water ahead.

I cleared my throat, excused us, and pulled Corellis with me. She glided like the graceful angel she was in the water. She was back in her natural element and thriving. The water melded to her body, clung to her skin. My nostrils flared at the emotions rising in my chest.

"Thank you, Yakobba," she said, looking up into my eyes.

I could get lost in those pools of blue. I floated closer, wanting to bear my hearts to her right there, but not finding the words to do so.

"You protected us, protected me. Yes, we have loss, but yours is greater. It may have been I alone who survived, if not for you. And the kindness you showed us while on your ship..." She looked around, struggling for words. At least I wasn't the only one having a hard time with reality crashing in. "In another world, in another life, maybe we... Thank you for everything, High Prince Yakobba. I won't ever forget you. And maybe... maybe one dawn, I won't have to."

Corellis flushed. My hearts raced. Before I could stop myself, I looped an arm around her waist, tugged her close, and crushed my mouth against hers. She tasted like the salty sea and fresh mint leaves that topped freshly brewed tea. My lips moved against hers, hungering for more. She fisted my tunic in her hands, tilting her head back, pressing herself into me. Skies. I could do this for a lifetime. But all too quickly, it was done.

We both cleared our throats, working to calm our breaths. When she looked up again, her eyes were bright with yearning, hope, and immeasurable sadness. What could plague her so badly?

"Thank you, my pirate prince. I won't ever forget you." Her last words were a broken whisper that wrenched me in two. Before I could say another word, she wormed her way out of my tight grasp, laughing to herself. Then she was swimming back to the Seaveillers, leaving me breathless and confused.

"We're here!"

I whipped around and gaped, my jaw hanging. Engèli had brought us to an open cove directly beneath King Au'Pearl's Pearl Palace.

CHAPTER 22
THE HUNT BEGINS
YAKOBBA

I watched Corellis and Kianga as they swam away. Corellis looked back once, pausing in the sea, looking at me with secrets buried in that knowing gaze I wished I had more time to learn. Then she turned away and the pair of them were gone.

I looked at Engèli, Nyala, Jabari, and Hezron. We floated on the deck, every angel already given their last orders.

"Remember," I said. "In and out. No noise, no trails."

"If there are bodies?" Engèli asked, a bit too excitedly. I groaned. He would never leave his El'Guard training dawns behind.

"If, and I do mean if, there are bodies," I shoot

him a flat warning glare. Engèli grinned, wriggling his brows, hand lovingly caressing the hilt of his cutlass."I already said it. No trails." My eyes flash at my best friend. "None, Gèli."

"I heard. Besides, I can't leave a trail," he said, a touch distractedly. "How will I come back to take Kianga for a... swim?" He grinned like a wolf.

Nyala and I snorted at the same time. Jabari shook his head, though he was wearing a grin, too. I'd caught him, more than once, finding a reason to be around the hardened Terfitti. Blessed skies.

"Hezron, you know what to do?"

The youngling nodded. "Keep quiet. Say as little as possible and act ashamed or full of pride. No in-between or else King Rhòdhaire and Prince Ishaèli won't buy it."

I nodded approvingly.

Hezron had a hard task to fulfill. He'd be disguised as me, going to the party of the king and entertaining himself, and others, as if he was the pirate prince they'd all heard so much about. Anything could go wrong. I told him to stay clear of mamè. If he so much as breathed by her, she would immediately know Hezron was a fraud.

"Alright, let's move. If the Alpha is on our side, we'll be back here in no time, having made no noise."

Another glare at a grinning Engèli. "Then we can get the rot out of here. Move!"

With a snap of my wings, every angel took off, flying in different directions. Sea angels were flying in and out, bustling around. This was the dawn the Avariens and Aziziens would meet, celebrate, then head to their Atlanthyst Trench for whatever solstice rituals they had planned.

I didn't give a rot about any of it. I needed to find the stone, take it, and get out.

Swimming away from the ship, I traveled out of the cave, through an empty reef, and out onto the grounds of the palace. It seemed as if every angel alive was here.

Thin, body clinging gowns with hanging pearls, shells, and jewels fell over the shoulders of ayèls, while the ayèn wore elaborate mesh-shirts and seaweed breeches. Almost all of them had a watery halo or small tiara perched on their head.

I glided towards them, letting the sea blue and green cloak around my shoulders blend in with the rest. Acting normal, I floated into the castle alongside them.

"Oh, I cannot wait to see the princess. She'll be beautiful!"

"I know! We didn't get to see her last cycle on her

riseday. I'm thrilled about this cycle. And on the dawn that she'll perform the Azizien Rite to save the kingdom!"

"Just like her mamè, that one! Beautiful as the stars, honorable as the sea. She'll put her duty first so our little ones can have a chance. Their generation won't survive the poisoned waters."

"But she is so young!" A strangled cry rang out. "Princess Raeshelle Corellis Au'Pearl hasn't even accepted a suitor. Built her life. See what the sea has to offer to her. Now she'll be sacrificed as some bloody offering to the sea. It isn't a Rite. It's murder! We have the Atlanthyst Stone, so we don't have to sacrifice princesses in its place! Princess Raeshelle Corellis deserves to live!"

"Oh shut up, bitter old croon!"

I froze dead on the spot, my blood freezing over.

Princess Raeshelle Corellis Au'Pearl?

My chest pounded as my mind screamed at me. But it couldn't be. Corellis was an Ayella-in-waiting. She waited on the princess. She wasn't the princess herself.

She couldn't have been the Ayella who'd been on my ship this entire time.

I thought of the Seaveillers. How Kianga shadowed her every step. Her courtly knowledge, posture, and grace. The Serène attack...

They hadn't come for us.

They were trying to cut us down to get to her.

She wasn't just Corellis. The Ayella-in-waiting had really been Princess Raeshelle Corellis Au'Pearl. The Pearl of the Sea. Dayè of the king. I thought back to the dawn in *the Crowned Bastard* and everything that unfolded after. Rotting ashes. It was her. Corellis was the princess! And according to these angels, not only this dawn was her riseday, but she was also going to perform an Azizien Rite.

My pearl, my Corellis, was going to die.

My chest twisted so badly I thought I would vomit. Skies! What was I going to do? I didn't come here for a rescue mission. I came here to steal the stone. The stone that should be used in this rotting rite so she wouldn't have to die.

Rot.

I wrestled with myself, feeling lost.

"Move out of the way, fish brains."

An angel rammed into my shoulder, shoving me out of the way so more guests could swim into the palace.

"I've never been to the Atlanthyst Trench before.

I can't wait to see it. And the pretty little princess that will be sacrificed in it."

Laughter swelled around me. I thought I was going to be sick. I didn't understand the ways of the sea. There was probably nothing to be done. For all I knew, she'd been prepared for this moment her entire life. It was probably the greatest honor of her life to do it. I forced down my queasiness. I had to concentrate.

Find the stone, get out of the palace, escape the sea.

I chanted the thoughts in my head over and over, despite feeling my body going numb. I couldn't help but see her two-toned blue eyes and her sweet smile. Hearing her laughter in my ears, I nearly doubled over again.

How was I going to do this?

How could I do this?

If I did, she would die!

But I had to.

I wanted to scream. Swallowing bile, I dashed down a separate hall from the partygoers. The hall was completely unguarded. I swam down its path, distancing myself from the angels in the palace. Soon I began noting details Aisha and Nyala had mentioned. I was currently in a corridor three halls away from where I would find the entry to the dungeons of the palace.

I briefly noted King Au'Pearl's wealth scattered throughout the halls. There were ornate tables, opulent tapestries, crystal carved chandeliers, and all kinds of fine details.

I swam with ease, thankful for all the lessons I'd been given. Too soon, I found myself before the door of pearls Nyala had once described. My pocket weighed heavily with the Atlanthyst Stone dupe. I looked around, making sure there was no one around to see me. The door was left unguarded. I looked around one more time, pried the pearl door open wide enough to fly through, and then slipped inside.

CHAPTER 23

DESCENT INTO DECEPTION

YAKOBBA

Darkness clung to the walls of the cavernous dungeon. The lights were dim. Small shell lamps littered the walls, helping with visibility. When I'd first spoken with Aisha, she'd shown me a map that was nothing short of marvelous. It was an intricate view of the underbelly of King Au'Pearl's palace. I would have to swim a long way forward, then swim downward, slipping through a narrow swimway that would bleed to a lightened corridor. From there, I would pass the dungeons themselves, which would lead out into the open cavern of the treasury. Swimming in this darkness felt like descending into the bowels of the Black Hells of Hayèl.

I swam languidly, noting every detail I could. There were an innumerable number of tridents hanging on the walls like unlit torches. Some paths led straight, while others curved back into darkness. I didn't plan on exploring. There was no sign of wear on the floors, which meant everyone who entered here only swam or floated.

As I began nearing the actual dungeon entry, closed off by another set of pearl doors, I heard three sets of shuffling.

"They'll be done with feasting and head to the Trench soon. We all have to go. King's orders. You know the princess is performing the Rite this cycle. Bakari wants everyone to see it. Just a little more of watching Azizi's filth and then we can go. Isn't that right? Avarien scum."

I realized then, one of those guards had to be speaking to an imprisoned angel from Avari. A part of me thought I couldn't leave the Avarien behind, but breaking Azizi prisoners out would earn me no points.

I swallowed my shame and kept swimming, keeping to the shadows to remain unseen. As I swam to my right, was the door hanging ajar with guards there. I kept my eyes on them as I slipped further into that narrow corridor, letting it take me in perfect silence before any of the guards could spot me. Once I was further down the corridor, a sound rose. I heard groans and screams coming from the belly of the dungeon. My chest pounded hard. If I'd stayed close any longer, I would've done something stupid.

It was eerily quiet down here. I kept my *ethèr* humming, and a hand on the hilt of my cutlass, in case anything tried impeding me from getting into that treasury. I probably should have come with Engèli, but he was needed elsewhere.

Even down in the bowels of the palace, I could hear the hum of excitement as the angels above, sea and sky alike, enjoyed themselves in raucous celebration.

A small part of me wriggled in envy. As a High Prince, I should be up there. Drinking, dancing, putting on a princely display for Avari. I'm sure Hezron was making a good show of it, but it should be me. Still, had I gone, mamè and Alessayi may have convinced me otherwise. It's one thing to suggest nabbing the Atlanthyst Stone while still in the Avarien castle. It was something else entirely to see it through when inside of King Au'Pearl's palace.

I swam through a stony archway that bled out into a deep cavern. I pulled up short. The first thing I noticed was the vastness of it. As if the rock could be beaten back for miles, still. The cavern was enormous, with hardened walls, hanging lines of crystal above, and shimmery pool depths beneath. I kicked my feet, floating above the waters that were separate from the sea itself.

The next thing that caught my attention was the majestic gate. Aisha had said it was a door. Nyala had confirmed it. Both had been wrong. The door was a gate and would need a trident to open. The gate was wide as the *Ashweaver*, and so high it nearly scaled the length of the cavern. Through a crease below it, I saw an ethereal glow.

The last thing I saw was a troop of Sea Watchers.

"Bloody ashes," I mumbled under my breath.

I knew a few had been summoned to overlook the festivities and be a safe escort to the Atlanthyst Trench for members from both kingdoms. But this. This was not something I expected. I came without Engèli thinking the coast would be clear.

"Rot." I ground my teeth, quickly counting them and noting there was no means of escape. I would have to fight my way through this one.

"If it isn't Captain Ashthorn, the pirate prince."

The Sea Watcher looked into my eyes, then spat at the water below her, disgusted. The warrior, covered in head to toe oceanic armor with seashells and pearls in gold trim, and a long trident in hand, stared at me, fury contorting her face.

"We've heard stories about you. I believed them to be searot."

She lazily seized me up and down, seeming unimpressed. Her accent was thick, just like Corellis. Rot. Not Corellis. Princess Raeshelle. My chest squeezed. I pushed the feeling aside and focused on the Sea Watchers.

"I suppose some were right," the Sea Watcher said. "You do look like a wandering vagabond."

I didn't take the bait. I grinned at her as I eased my cutlass out of its sheath and summoned my *ethèr*.

"You know, I'm an easier ayèn to deal with than most stories allude to," I said, still smiling. "Lay yourself down for me like the pretty little seastress you are, and I'd be happy to confirm a story or two."

The Sea Watcher snarled and charged.

I jumped out of the way, whipped out my *ethèr* like a long, flashing cord, and flipped over the Sea watcher. The lightning rope swept over her head, pulled her in, and bound her *ethèr*. Electric rope shocker her. The Sea Watcher screamed.

Then the rest charged.

There was fifty in all. I turned the battle into a dance. I swam with confidence like my sea counterparts, spinning myself in the water, swimming beneath the Sea Watchers and slicing their guts open.

There were a few of them guarding the gate while the rest rushed at me.

I didn't slow down, losing myself in the dance of death, swinging my cutlass.

I didn't have time for this. Skies only knew how much longer King Au'Pearl's guests would be entertained before going to the Atlanthyst Trench.

A swipe of blue steel cut across one of my wings, sending aching shocks throughout my body. I screamed, spasming with agony.

"Blessed rot!"

I couldn't get anything else out. Fighting through gritted teeth, I shoved the pain aside and forced my attention on the Sea Watchers swarming me.

With supernatural strength, I dove beneath them, swam outside of their circle, and before they realized it, I swiped and struck flesh, using my wings like they were cutlasses attached to my spine.

Blood filled the water as a Sea Watcher shot across and swiped their trident. I leapt out of the way. Another blow came and landed, striking my left shoulder. Gritting my teeth, I pushed through the pain. I roared and charged the onslaught. I swiped with my cutlass. Then I cut through fabric, skin, and bone with the sharpened edges of my wings. One by one, the Sea Watchers fell, including the troop who stopped barring the gate to the treasury to come and provide a defense. I used my cutlass like an extension of my arm until I was the last angel breathing.

I didn't have the time to siphon out their fôrs and kill them spiritually. For now, their physical deaths would buy me time.

When no one else stirred but me, spitting out a wad of blood, I swam to the crystal knobs.

"Blessed Alpha, I just want to say thank you. None of the bloody idiots had been smart enough to just break my etherisc. Had they done so, I wouldn't breathe any longer and the sea would have claimed me. I know I'm not in Temple often like I should be, but thank you for saving my hide, again."

Grabbing a floating trident, I shoved the tip into a triangular mechanism that seemed to have the same shape. It worked like a charm. The gate clicked, something on the other side popped, and the doors swung open.

When I looked inside, I whistled.

There were infinite mounds of jewels, precious stones, and gems.

"Let the hunt begin," I laughed. Then I flew into King Au'Pearl's treasury, fake Atlanthyst Stone in hand, and began my search for the real one.

CHAPTER 24
SHIELDING THE HEART OF ATLANTHYST
RAESHELLE

"Your payè isn't a fool. He won't fall for the decoy, Raeshelle."

Kianga trailed me through the quiet hall as we swam away from the rowdy party. We swam quickly, avoiding maydins and guests alike, lest they spread gossip and foil my plans. My gut twisted at the thought of betraying Yakobba, but I had no choice. I had to get to the stone first. If payè wouldn't give the stone to the waters of Azizi, then I would. I'd decided. I would not perform the Azizien Rite.

"I have a bad feeling about this," Kianga continued.

"Stop nagging or return to the feast!" I snapped.

I didn't have time for this. I was hunting for the

stone and I needed my concentration. If I knew King Bakari well, there were two places he'd put the stone. I opted for the first. The small chamber, carved from ancient rock, at the back of the treasury.

The problem was, I'd need to pass the dungeons to get to it. King Bakari had taken me to the treasury several times. He wanted to show me our wealth, but he also wanted me accustomed to challenging tasks. After all, one dawn I could be the one delivering an accused to the dungeons or have to fetch something from the treasury, he would say.

A cruel joke. He'd taught me all of that, knowing I'd put none of that knowledge to use. Well, it wasn't all useless. At least I could get to the dungeons. The only issue would be the guards.

"You know the king's wrath will spare no one, Raeshelle. Think about what you're doing and who it will affect."

I turned to look at Kianga. Her pretty face was hardened lines and creased with worry. She was right, of course. King Bakari could very well punish me and Kianga both, no matter what I said. And her punishment would be far worse.

But I wouldn't be deterred.

After watching all those angels laughing and dancing, excited, actually excited, for me to be given to the waters in the Atlanthyst Trench... I almost vomited. I decided in that moment; I was slipping out, nabbing the stone, and giving it instead. No punishment payè could give me would outweigh the fact that I could stay alive and eventually live my life. Yakobba had given me the taste of freedom and I wanted it badly.

"I will say this one last time."

I surged ahead, swimming with purpose. Kianga flinched, but listened.

"If you don't want to do this, then don't. I will face any blame or repercussions alone. But I'm not stopping, Kianga. The angels want me to die. They—"

I trailed off, unable to finish. I turned forward and swam faster. When I got to the pearl doors that would lead down to the dungeons, I froze.

"Look, I'm not saying they're right, because the bloody idiots are—"

Kianga broke off when she saw what I did. Not only was the door ajar, wide enough for a body to slip through, but the water smelled like an Avarien cloud walker. It smelled like him.

"Rotting seas," I cried in a small voice. "No, no, no!"

I was preparing to curse him for a thousand cycles.

Then it dawned on me.

I smelled him in the water, and only him. Which meant he swam down to the treasury alone. Fear now crept into my hearts for another reason.

"Kianga, he went down there alone. He may be..."

Kianga said nothing. When I looked at her, her relief was evident. If Yakobba went alone, it meant Engèli wasn't with him. Kianga met my eyes, then looked away, ashamed.

"I should help him," I began, looking at the door with uncertainty tying knots in my gut.

"But will you?" Kianga asked, knowing what was crossing my mind.

If Yakobba was down there, there was a likelihood the king knew someone, that someone being me, would go for the stone. Hence why there were no guards at this entry. Which only meant the stone was in the one other place he kept it.

I frowned, ashamed at myself. Yakobba could be down there, flying into a trap, and badly hurt. He would need aid, but I needed the stone.

He just wanted to impress his payè.

I needed to stay alive.

I looked at Kianga and blinked. She nodded, her

eyes grim. She understood, but it didn't mean either of us had to like the choice.

I closed the door so it would draw no more attention, then turned back down the hall, rushing through narrow corridors with Kianga in tow, flying fast for the king's wing. He should still be in the ballroom having a grand time. When I'd left, Prince Ishaèli was dancing with one of my Ayellas-in-waiting. He was graceful, and quite a fine dancer, even for an angel his size, but he was still a cocky-headed oyster who flaunted his power as if we should cower before it.

I'd been forced to dance with him.

I wanted to cut off my feet.

I had caught the mounting rage of King Rhòdhaire, and the nervousness of Queen Rekani, as their eyes scanned the ballroom hunting for a Yakobba I knew would never show up.

I flew down the halls distractedly. Kianga was speaking, but I heard nothing beyond the loud thump, thump, thump of my six racing hearts. I lifted a prayer to the Alpha, begging him to keep payè in the ballroom a little while longer.

I flew into the king's wing without a thought. I didn't look around, and really there was no need to. There were no maydins, guards, or nosey guests.

The halls and chambers had been deserted for the feast celebrations. Flying into the deepest part of his wing, swimming to the chamber where the king slept, I didn't hear Kianga until it was too late.

"Raeshelle!" Kianga screamed.

I stopped dead, my wings coming to a halt. In the slight pause, large, webbed hands clamped around my wrists and ankles. Chains of fishbone, metal, and reefwire were corded around them, and another around my neck, squeezing me tight. I spasmed, screaming out. When I screamed, the chain around my neck pressed into the column, breaking the skin. As blood trickled out, I stopped, already feeling tears pool down my cheeks.

"Raeshelle, my pearling. It shouldn't have to come to this. But you've always been so stubborn."

I snapped open my eyes to find King Bakari, with a band of his strongest Seaveillers, floating before me. Their wings flapped in the chamber as they watched me like I was a deep-sea bottom feeder.

"Looking for this, pearling?"

King Au'Pearl opened his palm. There, at the center, perched the Atlanthyst Stone in all of its power, glory, and beauty. My hearts twisted. I opened my mouth, a flurry of pleas tumbling out.

"Payè, please. Please. It doesn't have to be me. It

should be the stone. I'm your dayè. Does that matter for nothing?"

He looked at me for a long while, so long I didn't think he would speak. His eyes danced from me, then to the stone, and back. A small, cruel smile curled his lips. Evil darkened his eyes. Greed puffed out his chest.

"No, Raeshelle. You do not matter, because you're not enough. You have never been, and you will never be. Just like your mamè. How fitting for you to die in the same fashion. I'll relish your screams. The stone is mine and mine alone. It will not be given. You will be." He looked to the Seaveillers. "Take them to the hangar."

Then something hard clubbed me in the head and everything turned into a barren, endless sea.

CHAPTER 25
EXPOSED TREACHERY
YAKOBBA

Flying into the treasury, I stayed focused. King Au'Pearl's riches were impressive, but King Izakaya had much of the same in Avari. I opted to float, using my wings to help me navigate through the high mounds of treasures. It looked like a hoard for dargaen. It was said the scaly beasts would lecture you about trying to steal from them before turning around to flame you. Then they'd eat your wings. I shivered, staying away so I wouldn't touch anything by accident.

I looked through pile after pile, scanning over chests, cases, open boxes neatly arrayed between silver, gold, crystals, gems, precious stones native to the sea, and other coveted items. There were swords and cutlasses. Daggers, shields, and tridents. Spears, staffs, scaly chains, and even fishbone knuckles. There was much to be desired, but I wanted the stone.

"If I were a king planning to hide the Atlanthyst Stone, where would I put it?"

I looked to the far back of the cavern and began making my way there. I was impressed to see even more back here. Crowns, gowns, rings, necklaces, hooks, chains, goblets, and many treasures of the finest quality.

"What's this?"

I began swimming to an illuminated space. It was a small room only two or three angels could fit in comfortably. I drew close, mesmerized.

Premonition kicked in. Last time I didn't take heed, a troop of Sea Watchers were waiting for me. I began looking around and found I was alone. Smiling, I pressed in. This had to be where the king kept the stone.

I pulled out the Atlanthyst Stone dupe and neared the small arched opening. Pulling up to the light, I popped my head inside. There was an ornate chair, made of stone and seaweed, perched at an empty glass table. Beside the table was a stand. It was made entirely of gold and had a crystal case sitting on top of it. *ethèr* swirled around the case. I grinned, almost salivating. I'd finally found it.

The swirling mist cleared. When it settled, and I could see into the case, I snarled, raging in the small chamber.

The case was empty.

"Rotting burning ashes!"

I wanted to slam something until it shattered into pieces, much like how I felt.

"Where in the rot is this stone?"

If I was all the way down here looking for the stone, and it wasn't here, it meant someone knew that angels would try coming for it. Not just any someone.

King Bakari Ezrathen Au'Pearl.

If he had a hunch there would be a potential heist to nab the stone, where would he move the stone to? My brain felt pulled in a myriad of directions until one solution slammed me in the forehead.

"Bloody bastard took it to his chambers. He had to. Which means... rot."

I shot out of the small chambers, raced across the vast treasury, and began flying through the water to get back upstairs. My wounds screamed at me to stop, but I couldn't. I had lost so much valuable time and all for a farce.

"Rot!" I yelled again.

My throat ached. Sides burned as if on fire. My wings grew tired under the weight of the sea. It took much longer to get back to the main level from the treasury. I rushed past the dungeon, racing against time. When I reached the door, it was closed.

I pulled up short.

I knew for a fact I'd left it ajar. Now, it was closed. One cautious shove had it opening again. I began to think. Who had been here? Who knew I was down there?

Swimming out into the empty hall, I sniffed.

Salty sea and mint.

"Corellis," I blurted. Then my eyes narrowed. "No. Raeshelle."

I drawled the name, letting it come out nice and slow until I felt my body tingling with the heat that wasn't coming from my wounds. "You were here, weren't you, my princess?"

I smiled until I began laughing to myself. She was probably trying to get the stone herself. It's what I'd do. I looked around. It's almost like I could sniff her out. There was another scent that lingered in the air. It probably belonged to Kianga. That one never left Raeshelle alone. Raeshelle's scent was strong. It left me feeling heady. I wanted to shake it off and focus.

But I couldn't.

Something in me raged, twisting and turning, demanding I follow her scent now. Stupidly, I listened to that incessant voice.

Tracking by scent was a skill a past mentor taught me long ago. I'd used it for my first stay on Ashbone Island. Now, I navigated through the halls of the sea king's palace, following that trail of salty sea and mint. By the time I stopped swimming, I felt almost drunk from it.

"Payè, please!"

I sobered up fast. Blinking, I looked around me. I was in a hangar. From what I could see, it had stalls for underwater chariots and also sea beasts like seastallions. It would be nothing to fit a massive shrark in here. Skies. I prayed there weren't any. Shrarks had foul tempers. Slipping close to a low wall between the entry and the rest of the hangar, I crouched low, sneaking a peek over the wall to see who was there.

"Please, King Bakari. Please reconsider. It's Raeshelle! Your dayè!"

"Silence."

I flinched at the roar of the king. I knew what that was like. It wasn't fun being disciplined by a king.

"How could you give her up to die?"

That voice belonged to Kianga. She was yelling, but it sounded strangled. A garbled sound that made me shiver. I poked my head out and found there were two mammoth sized, all black shrarks in the hangar. Atop each were Raeshelle and Kianga. Both angels were chained around the neck, wrists, and ankles.

"I will say this one last time."

King Bakari addressed Raeshelle. For all he cared, Kianga was nonexistent. Seaveillers floated on either side of the harnessed, muzzled shrarks. I could feel my blood boiling. What in the rot was happening here?

King Bakari looked at Raeshelle with a coldness I had never seen in King Izakaya's eyes when he looked at me.

"Your mamè, Queen Audriana, was a pawn for me. And you, her spawn, are the same. I will admit, you surprised me. After all, you held more of the power from the Atlanthyst Stone in your body than she ever could. Ultimately, she could have lived. But Audriana was too weak to handle the power."

Raeshelle and Kianga gasped at the confession. I flinched.

Was King Bakari saying the queen didn't die from being given to the Mistwind Seas, but because he put too much of the stone's power in her body?

I felt myself shaking with anger.

"No matter how much I siphoned from the stone and fused into your body, you kept soaking it in. Truth be told, you could release the power from your body into the Atlanthyst Trench and survive it. But I won't be having it. You will release the power from your body, and then I will have your spirit drained."

A dark chuckle filled the hangar as I blinked back my shock. He was going to kill her. And for no good reason than his own greed. To keep up pretenses. She didn't have to die. He just wanted to put on a good show.

King Bakari smiled, cruel and vile. I ground my teeth, fisting my hands.

"Like your mamè, you will be given to the sea. I will retain my hold on the stone. Time will pass, your sacrifice will wane, I will bond again, sire seed, and they, too, will do the same. The kingdom will grow, my reign will not end, and the stone will forever be mine."

Like rot it would be. I would tear this entire

rotting palace apart before I left here without that stone and Raeshelle.

"Raeshelle Corellis Au'Pearl," the king said with finality. "I know it will be your honor to serve your king, and your kingdom, by giving your life to the Mistwind Seas."

Then he turned to the Seaveillers.

"I must be on my way. The Aziziens and Avariens have begun making their way to the Trench. As must I. Make sure she arrives after everyone. I want a grand entrance." His eyes flickered to Kianga. "Dispose of this one. I don't care what is around to lick up her bones after you dump her."

The king flew forward, mounted a seastallion that rivaled the shrarks in size, and galloped out of the hangar.

Raeshelle's body quivered. She cried helplessly. I could feel all six of my hearts breaking at once. I had a gut feeling King Bakari left without taking the stone. Which meant I could turn around right now and go find it. But then I'd be leaving Raeshelle behind and she would be killed.

I thought about the pride I would see on King Izakaya's face for the first time if I returned with the stone. The joy I would experience, finally feeling like his soè, not his bastard. I craved it so badly it made me ill.

But.

Raeshelle Corellis Au'Pearl.

The Pearl of the Sea.

Between Ashbone Island and now, she'd ensnared my hearts. I wanted to be nowhere, in no moment of time, without her. If I left her to be taken like slaughter, I'd never experience a dusk of peace again.

Pressing my lips together, I pushed my bodily pain to the recesses of my mind and tumbled into my wells of *ethèr*. I needed help of the supernatural sort. I swam in that well and watched the silhouette of my fôrs appear, the blazing light blinding.

"I need to save the Pearl of the Sea, but I can't alone. I need the strength of the Alpha to accomplish this."

The ethereal body of my fôrs floated in the light, shimmering in and out of sight. Unseeing eyes of light blinked once, twice, then the head nodded, agreeing. My fôrs spread out its arms and legs, then light exploded everywhere.

CHAPTER 26
SAVING THE PEARL OF THE SEA
YAKOBBA

The world was a brilliant, majestic landscape of ivory, lavender, and gold. The shards of effervescent light radiated everywhere I looked. I felt like I was floating through clouds. Everything felt unreal. Ethereal.

Endless explosions of power swelled through me, then out of me, without control. None of it was my doing. It wasn't my ability. I was just a vessel while my wells of *ethèr* burst violently, unmitigated power sloshing around liked an angry river, forcefully pouring out until, without warning, it all abruptly died down.

I blinked, slowly prying my eyes open, and found Raeshelle blinking down at me. My head was in her lap, while a wide-eyed, and to my amusement, very concerned Kianga, perched behind her. Their chains were gone, but I could see the marks the chains had left. I lifted a hand to Raeshelle's cheek, wincing at the pain. She nuzzled into my palm, brushing her fingers through my hair.

"My Pearl of the Sea," I croaked. "All this time, I was looking for the stone. And you, my beautiful, sharp-witted, gentle princess, were the stone the entire time."

I laughed, then wheezed. My body was wracked with pain. I could hardly breathe. My limbs were numb. Everything moved slowly. A warm, buzzing feeling bubbled in my gut.

Skies.

What had I done?

"Your chains..."

"Shh," she cooed.

I felt tiny droplets fall to my face. It took a moment to realize she was crying.

"You saved us." Her voice broke through her tears. "The Seaveillers. They all died. And the chains," she sniffled.

Behind her, Kianga's eyes glistened with tears.

"The chains melted away. They just dissipated. I only know it wasn't a dream because the scars remain. But you..."

Raeshelle's words abruptly cut off as she fell over me and sobbed.

Kianga pet her hair gently.

"You could have flown away, Yakobba. Learning the truth of who I was. Learning why I wanted the stone. The truth from the king. Seas. I can't even call him payè. You could have left. But you stayed. You fought for me. For us. I—"

She took my face in her hands, studying me through her tears. "You foolish, bullheaded, pirate prince. Why did you do it?"

"Because I love you, my pearl," I blurted out. "My head will end up on your payè's trident before I let you be taken from me."

She snorted, laughing. She looked so cute like that, her eyes bright and different shades of blue. Her ivory hair floating in the water. That salacious, pale blue dress hugging her in all the right places. I flushed, looking back into her eyes. Something else was there. Something that made me chill despite my aching limbs.

"Well, I suppose I love you, too. In the chaos, I found this had been left behind. I nabbed it for you."

From a fold I didn't know existed in her dress, Raeshelle slipped her hand in, then pulled out an iridescent stone. It was nearly the size of her palm, carved like a star, with running streaks of lightning that emanated a lavender glow. I jerked, flinching back from it.

"The Atlanthyst Stone." I looked up at her.

She watched me, amused.

"Do you not want it?" Raeshelle asked.

I snorted. "So you can be killed? Please."

"But your payè—"

"Has one soè he acknowledges exists." I looked away. "Maybe I'll have to accept that and let it be enough." I flickered my gaze to her. Her tears were returning. I couldn't stand it.

"Not you, my pearl. Never you," I whispered.

Then I mustered my strength, lifted from her lap, and kissed her. Hard, long, sweet. I moved in rhythm with her, our breaths becoming one until our tongues did their own dance. She was the sea to my sky, and I knew I would love her for a lifetime of lifetimes. When I pulled away, we were both shaking.

"I love you, my pearl."

Her eyes shimmered. I fought the temptation to take her lips to mine again. For Kianga's sake, I had to show some restraint.

For Kianga's sake.

"I love you, my pirate."

She kissed my cheek and dropped the stone into my palm.

"It is yours. It no longer belongs to Azizi, nor should it. It belongs to Avari, now. Bring it home, my pirate prince."

My chest squeezed.

"But you—"

"I will release the power from my body into the Atlanthyst Trench. Then I will do my best to evade King Bakari—"

I shoved the stone back to her.

"No."

"I mean, you could also release the power where the sea meets the sky, and let it heal the entire sea while you're far away from here. My payè taught me the power never had to be in the Trench. That's just for ceremonial purposes."

Raeshelle and I blinked at Kianga, who was brushing a strand of her hair behind her ear. She tossed an unimpressed look at Raeshelle.

"Some of us actually paid attention to our studies." She squared her shoulders, pressing on. "The stone was given in the Atlanthyst Trench. But the scrolls say it doesn't have to stay there. It can be used anywhere, so long as it is stored where it won't be harnessed, and used, for greed and selfish purposes."

Raeshelle snorted. "Like the king of the sea?"

Kianga grinned. "Kind of like that."

I butted in.

"So, I get to keep the stone of my hearts and the stone of the sea?"

My eyes widened. Raeshelle grinned.

"Only if we make it out of here before everyone comes back from the Trench."

I grinned back.

"I need to find Engèli and—"

"I'll find him," Kianga cut in quickly. "I'll find him and we'll meet you on the *Ashweaver*."

Before I could protest, she was gone.

I looked at Raeshelle. She only giggled.

"Those two have gotten... closer than we assumed."

I said nothing. Lost in her eyes, her scent, I was lost in everything that was her. I didn't want to leave her side, not for a moment, ever again.

"Well, my pirate prince," Raeshelle purred, pressing close until she was in my arms.

It dawned on me we were alone in this hangar. If I wanted to, I could claim her now. My cheeks burned as I shook the thoughts from my head.

"That was very inappropriate," she said, batting her lashes at me, as if she knew exactly what I was thinking. My cheeks burned hotter. "Will you take me home?"

Home.

Raeshelle meant the *Ashweaver*.

My chest knotted in ways that threatened to unravel me.

I smiled, leaned forward, and kissed her again. Slow and sensual, taking my time with every bite and breath. I relished in my Pearl of the Sea. The heart of my hearts. I squeezed her tight, feeling something in me settling into place. A sure feeling. A whole feeling. Something inside of me knit back together.

I kissed her again and again. Raeshelle, the princess of the sea, had entered my world, flipped it upside down, and left me in shambles. I peppered her with short, quick kisses until she started laughing. The sound had become my favorite to listen to.

"I adore you, my pearl," I sighed, leaning into her. Dropping the actual stone next to the fake one in my pocket, I gritted my teeth against my growing wounds, and rose to stand, keeping her lifted in my arms. I brushed a strand of her hair back and grinned like the luckiest angel in all the seas and sky. "Yes, my heart of hearts. Let's go home."

GLOSSARY

A lexicon with the definitions, translations, and interpretations found throughout Trapped By Pirates.

TRAPPED BY PIRATES GLOSSARY

Airflower (AIR-FLOWER): The ship captained and led by Captain Urnael Adekayi. Also a vessel of sentimental value to Yakobba Rhòdhaire, also known as, Captain Ashthorn, as this was a vessel he spent many years of his life wanting to captain and navigate but King Izakaya Rhòdhaire always denied his requests.

Airveiller (AIR-VAY-YER): Castle Guard. Interchangeable with soldier.

Aisha Faradhe (EYE-EE-SHA FAR-ADD): Crew member of the *Ashweaver*. Pirate.

Alessayi Favren Rhòdhaire (AL-LAY-SA-YEE FAVE-REN ROD-AIR): Princess of Avari. Younger sayè of High Prince Yakobba; Six cycles Yakobba's junior.

Alexra (ALEX-RA): Crew member of the *Ashweaver*. Pirate.

Alpha (AL-FA): God. The Almighty. The Great King. The Omniscient, Omnipotent, Omnipresent One.

Ashweaver (ASH-WEAVER): The ship captained and led by Captain Ashthorn, otherwise known as, High Prince Yakobba Izayi Rhòdhaire.

Astroproge (ASTRO-PRODGE): An angelic technological device which materializes landscapes, regions, angels, and any desired images from thin air, cloud, and *ethèr* to produce a clear, visual picture that can be viewed, analyzed, and used to communicate.

Atèmos (AH-TEM-MOS): Space; galactic atmosphere; the expanse in the outer universe surrounding the planets.

Atlanthyst (AT-LAN-THIS): An ancient underwater empire that was wiped from existence after the Taint poisoned the waters, and ultimately became the demise of the former empire.

Atlanthyst Stone (AT-LAN-THIST STONE): A smooth stone, shaped like a seashell that glows like a newborn star, with shifting pastel hues constantly changing its color and outer shine. Donned "Atlanthyst" Stone because it was given to the Aziziens amidst the Atlanthyst ruins, in the Atlanthyst Trench.

Atlanthyst Trench (AT-LAN-THIST TRENCH): A trench, or underwater valley, located at the bedrock of the former Atlanthyst empire. A body of ruins where the ethereal stone was first given and used to heal the waters of the sea from the Taint.

Audriana Deneise Au'Pearl (AWE-DREE-AH-NA DUH-NEESE OH-PEARL): Queen of Azizi. Former mate of King Bakari. Mamè of Raeshelle.

Avari (AH-VAR-REE): The sky kingdom located east of the Mist-wind Seas, above the Billowe separating the angelic kingdom from the Faeretheth kingdom of Norclère beneath the Billowe within the Zurethe planetary world. Filled with all kinds of sky-like, the Avari kingdom is mainly inhabited by angels of Domenent rank.

Ayèl (AH-YELL): The angelic term for *woman* or *female*.

Ayella (AH-YELL-LA): Ladies of angelic society. A respectful title of address for female angels.

Ayèn (AH-YEN): The angelic term for *man* or *male*.

Azizi (AH-ZEE-ZEE): The underwater kingdom located beneath the Mistwind Seas within the Zurethe planetary world. Filled with all kinds of oceanic beasts, the Azizi kingdom is mainly inhabited by angels of Domenent rank.

Azizien Rite (AH-ZEE-ZEE-YEN RIGHT): A traditional ritual where an angel with the power of the Atlanthyst Stone fused into their body releases the power into the waters of the sea. Survivable, but most often ends in the death of the angel.

Baere (BEAR): Bear.

Bakari Ezrathen Au'Pearl (BUH-CAR-EE EZRA-THEN OH-PEARL): King of Azizi. Mate of Queen AudrianaPayè of Raeshelle.

Bayè (BA-YEAH): *Brother* in the native language of Domenent angels.

Bedchamber (BED-CHAMBER): Bedroom. Also interchangeable with differing alcoves within an enlarged bedroom suite.

Bedcloud (BED-CLOUD): An angelic bed made entirely of clouds and ethereal matter.

Black Hells of Hayèl (BLACK HELLS OF HA-YELL):

Bond (BOND): An ethereal, living, golden cord, sometimes ivory, of life and power woven through the center hearts of angels that eternally binds the angels to one another for eternity and allows them functions such as, speaking to one another telepathically and sharing a measure of their *ethèr* with each other.

Bonding (BOND-ING): The act of marriage and eternal mating between angels which creates an eternal Bond between angels for their lifetimes.

Buckling (BUCK-LING): A vulgar insult. A bastard child easily abused and used for vile purposes.

Clam Lamp (CLAM-LAMP): A lamp made from clams.

Clipped (CLIPPED): Federal punishment for angels who have broken the law. Delinquent angels have every one of their wing pairs broken at the jointed points as clips of steel and *ethèr* are snapped into the former points of their wings rendering the angels disabled for eternity.

Cloudchair (CLOUD-CHAIR): A chair. Also interchangeable with a single-seater couch.

Cloumàk (CL-OW-MACK): A hammock.

Clouthren Harbor (CLOU-THREN HARBOR): A harbor port in the Avari kingdom.

Cloud Castle (CLOUD CASTLE): The castle of the king in the kingdom of Avari.

Condemned (CONDEMNED): The Fallen. Disgraced angels who were once Etheriens but have been stripped of their original order and been made into reprobate Fallen.

Coralsticks (CORAL-STICKS): Chopsticks.

Cosm (KOH-ZUM): Planet.

Cruesaiyi Reefsea De'Leau (CREW-SA-YEE REEF-SEA DEW-LOW): A siren. Was once a Domenent angel, grandchild of a former Azizien king, former cousin of Raeshelle Corellis Au'Pearl.

Cycle (PSY-CULL): One year.

Dakri (DAH-KREE): Crew member of the *Ashweaver*. Pirate.

Dargaen (DARE-GEN): A race of dragons who live in the Dèrn-eveil cosm and throughout the Caelesti realm.

Darkwing Kiss (DARK-WING KISS): A tavern in the Avari kingdom.

Dawn (DAWN): One day.

Dayè (DA-YEAH): *Daughter* in the native language of Domenent angels.

Dolfini (DOLL-FEE-KNEE): Dolphin.

Domenent (DOMINANT): A rank of angel in the Elledelle universe. The sixth rank of angelic hierarchy.

Dusk (DUSK): Night. Also interchangeable with evening.

Eelsilk (EEL-SILK): A fabric or textile found beneath the Mist-wind Sea.

Elector (ELECT-TUR): Teacher, professor, instructor, guide.

Elledelle (ELLA-DELLE): The universe in which the Elvriel realm and the Rèvaillèl cosm is located.

Ellelights (ELLE-lights): Eternity. Life beyond angelic death. Transition from the physical angelic plane to an ethereal, transcendent plane their spirits go to for all eternity.

El'Tide (ELLE-TIDE): The water solstice, water eclipse beneath the sea.

Engèli Ruakhe (EN-GELL-LEE ROO-AK): First Mate of the *Ashweaver* and quartermaster. Best friend of Yakobba Rhòdhaire. Pirate.

Ethèr (EY-THAIR): Innate, supernatural, magical powers of Etherien angels.

Etherisc (EH-THUR-RISK): A star-shaped clip. A small instrument that clips to the spinal column between angel wing pairs. When clipped on, an ethereal substance is released, allowing the angel to use the ability of the native angels. I.E. Sky Angels breathing underwater, or Fire Angels surviving in tundra-like climates.

Eya (EY-YAH): An expression of greeting or warning.

Fallen (FALL-LEN): Disgraced angels who were once Etheriens but have been stripped of their original order and been made into reprobate Fallen.

Firstfast (FIRST-FAST): Breakfast or the first meal of the day.

Fish Eater (FISH-EATER): A vulgar, insulting name for angels from the kingdom of Avari and Azizi.

Fishbone (FISH-BONE): A thread of bone made from the spines of varying fish.

Fôrs (FORCE): Angelic life energy and spirit. The spirit of angels is a distinct being that dwells inside of them, embodying their *ethèr*, able to communicate with the conscious of the host angel while fully submissive to commands given by the angel.

Frost Spring (FROST SPRING): Similar to a hot spring, where the steam is chilly as an iceberg and freezes anything placed within it to the point of shattering.

Hezron (HEZ-REN): Crew member of the *Ashweaver*. Pirate.

Hierrank (HIGHER-RANK): The title for angels of a higher rank.

Hôr (OARS): Hour.

Ifu (EE-FOO): Crew member of the *Ashweaver*. Pirate.

Imani (EE-MAH-KNEE): Crew member of the *Ashweaver*. Pirate.

Ishaèli Josiah Rhòdhaire (EE-SHA-ELLE-EE JO-SIGH-YUH ROD-AIR): High Prince of Avari. Twin and older bayè to High Prince Yakobba.

Izakaya Promeseren Rhòdhaire (EE-ZA-KA-YA PROM-EZER-REN ROD-AIR): King of Avari. Patriarch of the Rhòdhaires. Mate of Rekani. Payè of Yakobba.

Jabari Zarya (JUH-BAR-EE ZUH-RYE-YUH): Gunner of the *Ashweaver*. Pirate.

Jakran (JACK-REN): Crew member of the *Ashweaver*. Pirate.

Jaspen (JAS-PEN): Crew member of the *Ashweaver*. Pirate.

Jenessa (JUH-NESS-AH): A Seaveiller of Princess Raeshelle.

Karraba (KAH-RAB-BAH): Crab.

Kianga (KEY-UN-GA): A Seaveiller of Princess Raeshelle. Also, Princess Raeshelle's best friend and dayè to a Sea Lord of Azizi.

Kòd (COD): Cod fish.

Konda (CON-DA): A great serpent that walks, talks, and flies. A common form Fallen angels take on when shifting.

Lùne (LOONE): Moon.

Maergel (MARE-GUL): Mermaid.

Mamè (MA-MEH): *Mother* in the native language of Domenent angels.

Masaiya (MA-SIGH-YUH): Courtesan of the Darkwing Kiss.

Matteyo (MA-TAY-YO): A Seaveiller of Princess Raeshelle.

Mekàd (MAY-KAD): Month.

Millethium (MILL-LEH-THEE-UM): One thousand cycles.

Ministraithe (MINI-STRAIT-THE): The priestly order of the kingdom.

Mistwind Seas (MIST-WIND SEAS): Main body of water lying west of the Avari kingdom, located above the Billowe.

Monseriö (MON-SEH-REE-OH): A monstrous beast.

Naveren (NA-VER-REN): Owner of the Darkwing Kiss.

Nyala Tereth (NIGH-ALLA TER-RETH): Second Mate of the *Ashweaver* and arms master. Pirate.

Octocul (OCTO-KULL): A monstrous octopus.

Payè (PAH-YEAH): *Father* in the native language of Domenent angels.

Pearl Palace (PEARL PALACE): The palace of the king in the kingdom of Azizi.

Raeshelle Corellis Au'Pearl (RAY-SHELL CORE-ELLIS OH-PEARL): Princess of Azizi. Dayè of King Bakari. Pearl of the Sea.

Reefwire (REEF-WIRE): A kind of metal thread.

Rekani Allahiel Rhòdhaire (RUH-KA-KNEE ALLA-HEEYEL ROD-AIR): Queen of Avari. Mate of Izakaya. Mamè of Yakobba.

Rhèr (RARE): The vulgar, profane, way of saying buttocks or backside.

Rot (ROT): A vulgar term used to say poop, feces, and similar expressions.

Rotpot (ROT-POT): A derogatory term to call someone an idiot or a piece of rot.

Saelus Prison (SELL-US PRISON): An Avari federal max prison.

Saerel (SER-RUL): A rank of angel in the Elledelle universe. The third rank of angelic hierarchy.

Sayè (SA-YEAH): *Sister* in the native language of Domenent angels.

Scrypt (SCRIPT): The Holy Scroll. A sacred, holy compilation of scriptures Etherien angels live by.

Seaslugs (SEA_SLUGS): Underwater slugs found among bottom feeders of the sea.

Serène (SAY-REN): Siren.

Seastallion (SEA-STALLION): Seahorse.

Seastress (SEA-STRISS): A mistress. Interchangeable with courtesan or harlot.

Seavine (SEAVINE): Vines made out of seaweed.

Seawine (SEA-WINE): Wine found and indulged in under the sea.

Seedling (SEED-LING): An infant. Interchangeable with toddler.

Seaveiller (SEA-VAY-YER): Castle Guard. Interchangeable with soldier.

Se li se okea. Touye yo heidät kaikki. Li se on minun. She is the one. Kill them all. She is mine.

Sea Watcher (SEA-WATCHER): Warrior. Interchangeable with soldier.

Shellchair (SHELL-CHAIR): A chair. Also interchangeable with a single-seater couch.

Shell Lamp (SHELL LAMP): A lamp made from shells.

Shrark (SHRUH-ARK): Shark.

Skyfuel (SKY-FUEL): A type of fuel sourced in Avari that acts like oil and gas to power transportation vehicles throughout the kingdom, such as ships, chariots, etc.

Soè (SO-EH): *Son* in the native language of Domenent angels.

Sòl (SOLE): Sun.

Sôlight (SOLE-LIGHT): Sunlight.

Sôlset (SOLE-SET): Sunset.

Solstice (SOLE-STICE): A specified time each cycle when the trilùnes and sôlsunes cross causing a longer day than usual. A time when the angels celebrate the going year and lavishly usher in the new year.

Sôlsunes (SOLE-SOONS): Suns.

Soulu (SOUL-YOU): Mate. Interchangeable with spouse.

Starcrystal (STAR-CRYSTAL): A kind of metal.

Stingspray (STING-SPRAY): Stingray.

Sumaren (SUE-MA-REN): Submarine.

Swimway (SKY-WAY): Highway in the sky, usually above the clouds.

Terfitti (TER-FEE-TEA): A Seaveiller of Princess Raeshelle.

The Crowned Bastard (THE CROWNED BASTARD): A tavern in the Avari kingdom, mainly frequented by royals.

Tobe (TOE-BEE): A Seaveiller of Princess Raeshelle.

Tombabi (TOME-BAH-BEE): An Avari Airveiller.

Trok (TROK): Orc.

Tuana (TWO-AH-NA): Tuna.

Tunde (TOON-DAY): An Azizien Wheel Ryder.

Turtu (TUR-TWO): Turtle.

Urnael Adekayi (Ur-nay-ul AH-DAY-KA-YEE): Captain of the Airflower.

Votre payè était yon moun fou, annoit sinun kite wayòm nan. Maintenant, vous aurez saat maistaa, mitä hän teki sa li te fè nou. Your payè was a fool for letting you leave the kingdom. Now you'll get a taste of what he did to us.

Warstallion (WAR-STALLION): A horse, steed, or stallion typically owned by royals or the military often born and bred for war.

Waterway (WATER-WAY): Highway below the sea. Can be through pods of fish and inhabited reefs, or far out in the sea, away from sea life, but leading directly from the sky kingdoms to the sea kingdoms.

Wèk (WEH-K): One week.

Wheel Ryder (WHEEL-RIDER): A chariot driver.

Yakobba Izayi Rhòdhaire (YAH-KO-BA EE-ZA-YEE ROD-AIR): High Prince of Avari. Soè of King Izakaya and Queen Rekani. Twin and younger bayè of High Prince Ishaèli. Captain of the *Ashweaver*. Fearsome pirate prince.

Youngling (YOUNG-LING): Young angel. Interchangeable with adolescent or teenager.

Zukon (ZOO-CON): A Seaveiller of Princess Raeshelle.

AUTHOR'S NOTE

Fellow Etherien,

I'm so grateful for you. Thank you for taking the time to read **Trapped By Pirates.** I hope you loved reading it as much as I loved writing it. If you enjoyed this story, would you mind **taking a moment to write a review on your preferred reading platforms**? A few words on how you felt about the story will help me in more ways than you know. Thank you! See you in the next adventure.

Continue your journey: stephaniebwabwa.com

THE ADVENTURE CONTINUES

I hope you loved Yakobba and Raeshelle as much as I do. If you're hungry for more, no worries there. Another romance like this is in the universe. If you're ready for more, visit: **stephaniebwabwa.com** to find your next adventure. Until next time, see you in Elledelle.

- Stephanie

READER NOTE

Dear Etheriens,

For your convenience, you'll find a glossary towards the back of this book to help you with pronunciations, definitions, and translations.

Wings high! Enjoy the tale.

— Stephanie

ALSO BY STEPHANIE BWABWA

Of Seas and Tides

Trapped By Pirates

The Ethereal Kings

Barbarian of the Stars

Starry Kingdoms of the Fae

Bound By Watchers

Legends of the Obedayas

1. The Beginning of All

2. Summons of the Realm

3. Journey Into the Realmway

4. Monsters Hidden In the Void

ABOUT THE AUTHOR

Stephanie BwaBwa is a Christian, Afro-Caribbean, Epic Fantasy and Swoon Author. She's the Founder and author behind Elledelle: a universe filled with angels, adventure, romance, and light. A plurilingual Canadian of Haitian and Congolese descent, she's a lifelong reader, turned writer, turned author. You can usually catch her lost in her creativity with too many snacks. Get in contact with Stephanie directly at: **www.stephaniebwabwa.com**.